KEY to the DREAM

C. J. Johns

WALDENHOUSE PUBLISHERS, INC.
WALDEN, TENNESSEE

Key to the Dream

This is a work of fiction. Names, characters, places, and incidents either are the products of the author's imagination or are used fictitiously. Any resemblances to actual persons, living or dead, businesses, companies, events, or locales is entirely coincidental.

ISBN: 978-1-947589-89-6
Published by Waldenhouse Publishers, Inc.
100 Clegg Street, Walden, Tennessee 37377 USA
www.waldenhousepublishers.com
1-812-549-7536   1-424-886-2721
Cover painting by Carolyn Riddle
Type and design by Karen Paul Stone
Library of Congress Control Number: 2025915556

    A story of true love, and years of amnesia leading to a
    very dark place in search of the past. Fate intervenes for
    a surprise ending. -- Provided by publisher

FIC000000 FICTION / General
FIC022000 FICTION / Mystery & Detective / General
FIC027110 FICTION / Romance / Suspense

DEDICATION

To my family, with all affection.

CONTENTS

PREFACE

A beautiful young woman settles in a new town. She quickly makes friends. She meets her soul-mate, a preacher's son, and soon they are married.

All is perfect until ... While away from home alone, he is found, bloody and beaten, on the side of a road by an elderly couple. Once the couple realize he had NO MEMORY, they take him in as their own. For years, he searches for his past. The search almost breaks him, leading to a very dark place.

But ... what does fate have in store?

WHAT READERS ARE SAYING

"Compelling. A Page Turner"
   P. A. Riddle, Architect, Bradley County, TN

"Key To The Dream is captivating. I loved each of the characters. Looking forward to the next chapter."
   P. L. O'Neal, Special Education Teaching Assistant

"Romance - Tragedy - Drama! It has it all."
   Coleman Riddle, Retired Olin Chemical

"I wanted more. Can't wait for a sequel."
   K. Mull, Financial Executive, Baltimore, Maryland

"A great summer read."
   D. J. Benson, member of Choctaw Nation of Oklahoma

ACKNOWLEDGMENTS

I could not have written this book without encouragement and help from my family and friends.

My dear daughter and spell checker, Joy; my sweet daughter-in-law, Paula for many hours of typing; my son, Bill, for his humor; my son, Paul who named me 'A BEST SELLING AUTHOR'; my good friend, Kellye, who gave me inspiration, and my precious granddaughter, Stephanie, for her enthusiasm.

CHAPTER ONE – PRESENT DAY

Angel, my golden retriever, woke me. She was whining and prancing up and down. I knew what that meant. I glanced at the clock; it was mid-morning. I had overslept. It had been a restless night. Something was bothering me that I couldn't quite put my finger on.

I got up and padded through the house bare-foot, took a step into the kitchen and turned on the coffee maker. I slid open the patio door and watched Angel make her way down the steps. I watched as she did her business then patrolled her territory, sniffing every critter that had passed in the night.

It was a beautiful September morning. A slight breeze moved the remaining crepe myrtle blossoms on the huge trees. The river behind the house was as still as glass, barely casting a reflection. I heard the coffee maker gurgle that it was ready. I poured a cup and called Angel in. I had a busy day and couldn't take time for breakfast.

Angel came in, brushed my leg and stopped, whining and cowering behind me. She was looking toward the darkened living room. Just then I heard a creak in the old floor. My heart skipped a beat. I took a couple of steps, squinting to see. What I saw made goose-pimples all over my body. It could only be described as a HUMAN SCARECROW!

Instinctively, I threw the cup of coffee and hit him on his chest, screaming as loud as I possibly could, although there was no one to hear me.

It startled him enough for me to make a dash for my phone on the dining table. Just as my hand closed on it, a firm hand gripped my wrist. I looked directly into sick, green eyes, and he croaked out, "Don't Faye, don't. It's me, Zach."

He barely got it out when his eyes glazed over and he slumped to the floor, almost taking me with him. My mind was racing.

Was I going crazy? Was I having a nightmare or a breakdown?

I stepped away and watched to see if he was breathing. He was, but he was definitely unconscious.

The eyes and voice were somehow familiar, but it couldn't be Zach. Zach was my husband. He drowned over two years ago while fishing alone, and his body was never recovered.

This man was barely breathing.

While keeping an eye on him, with trembling hands I got the 911 operator and realized I was screaming, "This is Faye Hollister, 100 Windmill Lane, a man broke into my house and is lying on the floor, maybe dying." I ran to the bedroom, Angel right behind me. Keeping an eye on the door, I opened the nightstand drawer and felt for Zach's .38 caliber, detective special.

I remembered he had told me, "It's loaded-all you have to do is pull the trigger and aim for the chest."

I laid it on the bed and pulled on yesterday's jeans and t-shirt, slipped on sandals and picked up the revolver. Angel was hiding under the bed, so I closed the door behind me to keep her safe. I heard the sirens screaming onto Windmill Lane.

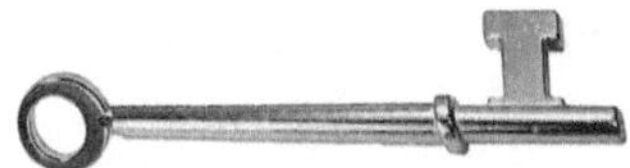

CHAPTER TWO –
FORTY MONTHS EARLIER

I could hardly believe that I, Faye Hawkeye Dobbs, 20 years old, was leaving everything I had ever known.

I was on Interstate 40, everything I owned crammed into Mama's old Chevy Monte Carlo. I told myself, "I'll just drive east and when I come to a place with big trees, water and rolling hills, I'll stop and see what happens."

I am one quarter Choctaw, born in the territory to Oscar and Dorothy Dobbs. I'm an only child and it's a good thing. My life wasn't easy, but I managed to graduate high school with honors. My dad cut fence posts and other lumber for a living, when he wasn't drunk.

Mama was a cook in a casino as long as I could remember.

I went to work there, too, before I was out of school, waiting tables and making good tips from the gamblers. I was saving all I could and counting the days 'til I could leave and see what else was out there.

Dad was a mean drunk, especially to Mama. Sometimes he would bully her and push her around until he got her payday. He would then go to his favorite hang out and buy drinks for his buddies, until nothing was left for rent.

I would give the landlord what I had and promise, "Mama will pay when she gets her check." I grew up way too fast, having to be an adult, when I just wanted to hang out with my friends.

It all came to an end four months ago.

Dad came in, falling down drunk, asking Mama for a hundred dollars. She told him she didn't have it, and he either pushed or knocked her into the old rock fireplace. She hit her head and never regained consciousness.

She died two days later.

Tribal justice is swift. Dad was found guilty and sentenced to life.

I did hug him goodbye.

I talked to Mama's sister, my Aunt Jessie. She said, "Honey, I don't blame you for wanting to see the world."

She held me and said into my hair, "Be careful, keep in touch, and have a wonderful life."

I sold Dad's portable sawmill and his tools, his old pickup and tractor, our furniture and Mama's hand-made blankets – all but the one she made for me.

Neighbors came and bought dishes and clothes. Everything was cheap. I needed enough to take me somewhere for a new start. I called my girlfriends and my boss at the casino and said my goodbye's.

And now, here I am, thinking how fast my life is changing, a little excited and a whole lot scared.

I didn't have much experience driving on the interstate, so I stayed in the right lane, never going over the speed limit and besides, I couldn't push the old Monte Carlo.

It had been almost noon when I took my last look around the old house Mama rented for years, the only home I could remember.

I couldn't help shedding a tear as I drove down the old road.

I got off of an exit about four o'clock to fill up with gas and go to the bathroom. I picked up a bar of candy and asked the clerk, " How far to the next town?"

She said, "About sixty miles to a real town." I decided that's where I'd stop for the night.

I noticed an older man looking me over. I knew I was pretty. I was crowned "Choctaw Princess" two years in a row. Maybe I shouldn't have worn short shorts, but it was hot, and I couldn't depend on the old car's air conditioning.

When I got in my car, I immediately locked the doors.

When I pulled out, he pulled out behind me.

He was following me. My heart was racing, what to do, what to do? I had nothing to protect myself but a flashlight. So I slowed to forty miles an hour. He slowed too, now right on my bumper, waving for me to pull over. He followed me for twenty miles. Suddenly, I saw a highway patrol car at an exit and turned off without giving a signal. He sped off. I pulled over and cried a little, trying to calm myself. What had I gotten myself into?

I sat for several minutes, then said aloud, "Faye Hawkeye Dobbs, you're on your own, be an adult."

I pulled back onto 40. I did stop at the next town, Melbourne, got a room at a cheap motel and got out my driver's license.

When the desk clerk, an older man, looked at my license, I knew what was coming.

"Yes," I said. "My name is Faye Hawkeye Dobbs. My mama named me Faye for her mama and my dad named me Hawkeye. He said as soon as I was born, my black eyes were looking everywhere."

I went across the street and got a sandwich and a Coke and took them to my room. I double locked the door and put a chair under the door knob. I had never been away from home. I turned the TV on. It was boring, local news. I ate my sandwich, looked in the shower, thought about it, and decided to wait until morning when people were moving about.

I realized I was still shaken from the stalking incident. I finally went to sleep after checking to see if my money was still in my luggage. I dreamed of Mama.

I woke myself up crying.

I had some cereal and a donut in the motel area, took a banana in my purse and checked out. I looked inside the car before I got in.

I'm nervous now - I'm alone.

I saw the ramp to get me back on 40 and I was off, thinking, *I'll make good time today, maybe I'll find THE PLACE.*

However, after driving nine hours, I repeated last night. *This is my second day, I don't think I want to travel much further,* I thought.

Around two o'clock, I was hungry. Soon I saw a sign, "Cloverdale Exit 25 'A GREAT PLACE TO LIVE.'"

"I just hope it's a great place to eat," I said aloud. A country diner was right off the exit. I had country fried steak, mashed potatoes and green beans. That was Mama's specialty at the casino.

"Do you live here?" I asked the waitress.

"All my life. I wouldn't live anywhere else," she replied. I bought a paper on my way out, *The Cloverdale Daily.* I decided, since it was early, I would drive around the town.

After all, there are plenty of hotels if I need to spend the night. I tried to keep track of my directions, and drove downtown, first. *It's the usual,* I thought. A courthouse, stores, a movie theater, museum, several eating places, and a lovely shaded park with a big gazebo.

A few blocks out was a good sized community college, what I was looking for. The streets nearby were shaded by huge, old trees and the lovely old homes were at least a hundred years old. I drove further out of town where subdivisions covered several miles. There were mountains on the horizon and a beautiful blue river. I felt something in me tug and decided to spend the night.

I never left.

The next morning, I asked the desk clerk if he knew of a safe place to get an apartment.

He grinned and said, "Well, she's kinda my competition, but Mabel Daniels bought a place about three blocks behind the college. She only rents to women, calls it Daniels Rooming House."

It was a good place to start.

I had no trouble finding it. It was a two-story apartment building, about six rooms on each floor. It had been white-washed, and the grounds were neat. The sign said. "Single women only."

Mrs. Daniels was dusting around in the lobby. It had plenty of seating and a big screen TV. She looked up at me, and I introduced myself. Mrs. Daniels had a good chuckle at my name. She showed me one of only two rooms she had empty. It was on the second floor with no elevator. There was a microwave, tiny refrigerator, and a coffee maker. The bed and bathroom looked decent. It had recently been painted, the palest olive green. I tried the small TV. It was OK.

I told Mrs. Daniels, "I'll take it – if I can afford it."

She said, "Wait a minute, Faye Hawkeye. I have rules." She was serious now. "No smoking, no overnight guests, and no men past the lobby. Oh yes," she continued, "no hot plates allowed."

I said, "That's all fine with me Mrs. Daniels," and paid for one month. That would be plenty of time to make sure this is 'THE PLACE'. I asked Mrs. Daniels where the nearest bank was.

She said, "Cloverdale National is on the east side of the courthouse."

I unpacked just what I needed for now. I made sure the door was locked and unpacked the old suitcase with my cash. I had just a little over five thousand dollars. I had plans now. I wrapped exactly five thousand tightly in an old scarf and stuffed it in the very bottom of my purse. I had no problem finding the bank. In about thirty minutes. I, Faye Hawkeye Dobbs, had a checking account, something my family never had.

A newspaper stand was outside the bank. I bought one and sat in the car reading help-wanted ads. *Tomorrow*, I thought, *I'll dress up and try to get an interview or two.* Since it was early, I decided to walk around downtown.

Cloverdale is just about perfect, I thought. A beauty shop, boutique, drug store and specialty stores. The drugstore had an old-fashioned lunch counter. I hadn't eaten anything today. I chose a stool and ordered a BLT and coffee. A large Coca-Cola calendar on the wall behind the counter read "August 21." With a jolt, I realized, In two days I will be twenty-one years old. So much had happened this summer. Time had flown so fast.

Mama always celebrated my birthday. Maybe just a homemade cake and school clothes. She would make a freezer of ice cream and invite Aunt Jessie and her three children, my only cousins. We would run around the yard playing tag or Choctaw stick ball.

I was lost in my memories, then noticed the clerk waiting to be paid. "Could you direct me to a grocery store?" I asked her.

It wasn't far, just two signal lights from the railroad tracks. I bought a quart of milk, bread, cereal, peanut butter, Oreos and two frozen dinners. When I got back to Mrs. Daniels, some of the roomers were visiting in the lobby. I guessed they were just off work. I got my groceries up the stairs. *At least it's well lit,* I thought.

I went back to the Monte Carlo and gathered what belongings I could carry and made sure the doors were locked. As I came in, Mrs. Daniels stepped from her apartment in the rear, I could smell something delicious cooking.

"Some of the girls gather in the lobby in the evening and visit or watch a movie. You're welcome to come down," she told me. She called out, "Brenda, Robin, Phyllis, come meet Faye."

I sat my load down and shook hands.

Phyllis said, "We all work at the chair factory. We get off at three-thirty."

Brenda asked, "Where do you work Faye?"

I replied, "I'm new in town, I'll be looking for a job beginning tomorrow."

Robin spoke up, "Hey, you can get on at the factory. They are always hiring."

I said "Thanks, Robin, but I'll have to work part-time. I'm going to college."

They were quiet for a moment, then Phyllis said, "That's great, Faye, come down and join us after a while."

"Thanks, but I have to get settled in and be ready for job-hunting early in the morning," I told them, "But, I'll be down one night. It was nice meeting y'all."

I gathered up my bags, struggling to hold them when Robin took one from my hands.

"Here, Faye," she said, "You look plumb tuckered out."

I turned the TV on, unpacked and put my things in the dresser drawers and the small closet. I hung a pair of brown slacks and a cream colored blouse over the chair. I thought, *That's perfect for the interview.* I watched early news, paying special attention to news around Cloverdale. It was typical, a musical at the college, high school football was beginning, a festival at the senior community center.

I realized I was bone tired, took a shower, had a peanut butter sandwich and a glass of milk and crawled into bed. I couldn't go to sleep for a long time, thinking about my trip, how quickly I had found what seems to be a good, safe place for now. I dreamed of a long-ago birthday.

The next morning, I took special care with my make-up and hair. My hair is long, with natural waves and curls. It really does what it wants. I checked myself in the mirror one last time, picked up my purse and said aloud, "Well, Faye Hawkeye Dobbs, the world awaits."

It was only three blocks to the college. I decided it was easier to walk than look for parking. Fall Semester was starting and after waiting in the line for awhile, I registered for two evening classes, computer science and advanced social studies and told myself, "One day I'll be a teacher."

I went to the used book store and bought what I needed. I already had a laptop. *Now to find a job to fit my schedule*, I thought. I had two to check out, both in a shopping mall north of town. The first one was a chain drug store, working in the pharmacy evenings and weekends.

The other was a department store, also with hours I couldn't do. I drove around a while, checking out the north side of Cloverdale. The more I saw, the more at ease I felt. I bought today's paper and drove back to Mrs. Daniels'. I thought to myself, *I may as well call it home,* and I did.

I changed my clothes into shorts and a t-shirt, laid across the bed on my belly and read the local news – who died, who got married, who had a baby and who was arrested with a picture of "Eric Stroud, crime and court reporter. " I could hear the buzz and laughter downstairs.

Maybe I'll go down after-while, I thought.

But, I didn't. I read the help wanted ads and got excited. One ad was meant just for me. It read, "Part-time server needed at Don's Steak House. Must be experienced and able to work ten a.m. until two p.m. See Don before ten a.m., across from the south side of the courthouse." I was there at nine-thirty. I introduced myself to Don and his wife, Penny. Don asked for a reference. I gave him my manager's name and number at the casino and told him I worked there for three years.

Don looked me over and said, "Penny will get you a uniform in a minute, but first get acquainted with our menu. He handed me a menu with a denim-looking cover. It was pretty standard.

Penny said, "Let's go in the back, young lady, and see if we have something to fit you." The uniform was denim shorts and a vest with "Don's Steak House" on the back. Penny said, "That looks close enough, now tie your hair in the back."

My heart was racing when the first customer came in at ten twenty. Suzanne, the other waitress, I guessed her to be about thirty-five years old, said, "Get your feet wet kid. Here comes the biggest lawyer in town for his usual coffee and bagel. Go get him."

The four hours went quickly by. Most customers came for lunch. Suzanne clued me in on the usuals. There seemed to be lots of lawyers, clerks from the courthouse and young business men and women having two-hour lunches.

Most people asked, "Where are you from?" and welcomed me.

About two-ten, Don said, "Well, what do you think, Faye Hawkeye Dobbs? I called the casino and the manager gave you rave reviews. Do you think this is what you want?" he asked.

I said, "Oh, it's exactly what I want since I'm taking evening classes. Do I have the job?"

"As long as you want," Don answered. He smiled. "Penny said you're a natural and received lots of compliments from the customers. You're hired," he grinned. "Can you start tomorrow?"

Don looked to be in his sixties, bald with a short gray beard, blue eyes, not much taller than me. I smiled, "Terrific, best birthday present I could have."

"Oh," Don said, "Why didn't you say something? I'll have Carl fix you something to eat. You must be empty."

"Thanks, Don. You and Penny have really made me feel welcome. I am a little hungry. I'll have a club sandwich and a Coke."

In no time, Carl brought my food out himself. He was the head cook, fat with a big grin. We had met briefly. "Here little girl, Happy Birthday and welcome to Don's Steakhouse and to Cloverdale," he said.

I went home tired, but happy. Showered, put on lounging pants and a tee. Just as I was brushing my hair, the phone rang. It was Mrs. Daniels, "Could you come to the lobby, Faye?" she asked.

"Sure," I answered. "Be right there."

As I went down the stairs, I smelled a wonderful aroma. I entered and saw several women seated around the lobby.

Mrs. Daniels was coming from her apartment with a huge platter of warm chocolate chip cookies. "Happy Birthday," she called out.

"How did you know?" I gasped.

"I saw your driver's license, remember?" she smiled. Suddenly, they were all singing, "Happy Birthday to you."

I met some of the roomers I had not seen before, including a young woman about my age with a broken nose and two black eyes. It seems Mrs. Daniels keeps a room for women trying to escape an abusive relationship.

"I have my favorite movie for anyone who wants to stay," Mrs. Daniels announced. When Steve Martin's, *The Jerk* started, we all began laughing and didn't stop until the end. We ate every last cookie crumb and hugged one another like sisters.

I thanked Mrs. Daniels again and went up to bed, thinking *I'm home.*

At Don's, I was learning the regulars. Some came in every day. One I recognized, "Eric Stroud, crime and court reporter." By my third week, he sat at my station regularly, always wanting to talk and leaving a good tip.

My classes had started. I just had time to shower and dress after work. I walked to the college when the weather was good. I thought, *When the days get shorter, I'll drive and not walk alone after dark.* I was always aware of my surroundings.

One day after work, I saw the back of a tall man loitering near the Monte Carlo. I slowed, thinking, *What will I do? Get Don or Carl to walk with me?* I was about to turn around when the man turned around, smiled and waved. It was Eric Stroud.

I said, "Hi, am I committing a crime?"

He grinned, "Oh no, I didn't mean to startle you. I just wanted to chat for a minute."

I said, "Well, chat."

He said, "Well, uh, I don't know hardly where to start."

I have always been very direct, so I said, "Then start at the beginning."

He looked at the ground for several seconds, then raised his head and looked at me very seriously. I didn't know what to expect.

"You don't have that much time, so I'll introduce myself. I'm Eric Stroud." He went on, "I work for the newspaper. I'm twenty-six years old, divorced with a son, Everette, who is almost four years old." He went on, "You can ask anyone about me, I'm just an average guy, trying to ask you on a date."

I hadn't dated much since high school. I looked at him for a long minute. He was nice looking, tall and lean, reddish-blonde hair, blue eyes, clean shaven and neatly dressed. He was staring at me, his face slightly red.

I finally said, "I know who you are. Where do you want to take me?"

He stammered, "Uh, where do you want to go?"

"I don't really know what's here to do," I answered.

He said, "Do you like to bowl? There's a great bowling alley near Shady Grove Mall."

I laughed and told him, "I've never bowled. But, I have to get to my class now, so I'll tell you when you come in for lunch tomorrow."

His shoulders seemed to relax. He grinned and opened the car door for me. "Can't wait for tomorrow," he smiled. "Please don't disappoint me."

When I came in that night, Mrs. Daniels was alone, watching TV. I told her Eric Stroud had asked me out. "Do you know anything about him?" I asked.

"Oh yeah, he's a good guy, never heard any bad talk about him. His folks had a dental practice for years. They retired and moved. He married Karen Beck, but it didn't last long," Mrs. Daniels assured me. "Are you going out with him?" she asked.

"Well," I said, "just bowling. Thanks Mrs. Daniels. Good night."

The next day Eric came in a little early. I could smell cologne as I took his order. "Don't keep me hanging, Faye. Am I the luckiest guy in Cloverdale or not?" he asked.

I answered him with a smile and said, "I have to study for an exam on Saturday, but I can go Sunday afternoon."

He almost shouted, "Woohoo!"

I said, "Pick me up at Daniels Rooming House at about four. I'll be in the lobby."

The bowling alley was busy. It was only the second time I had been in one. Eric got our shoes and selected a ball for himself and gave me a demonstration. He was pretty good.

The ball was heavier than I thought. When I turned loose, I went with it. Everyone around us was laughing as Eric picked me up. I don't give up easily, but I just couldn't get the hang of it.

We had a good pizza and Eric told me that he gets Everette every other weekend from ten Saturday morning until six Sunday evening. "Would you like to meet Everette next week?" He asked.

I said, "It's a date."

Eric seemed so excited, I thought, *I had better go slow with this one.*

The week went quickly with Eric in Don's everyday as usual, happy and kidding around. On Sunday, he picked me up, and Everette was in the back in his car seat.

Eric said, "Hey, Everette, this is Faye. She's a friend of mine and she's an Indian. Everett's eyes widened. He looked at me but didn't speak.

Eric said, "She's going to play in the park with us." Still no response from Everette, who was holding his red sand bucket and shovel. He finally glanced at me and stuck out his lower lip.

In the park, Everett wanted to slide and yelled out, "Daddy, it's burning my legs, swing me." Soon, he let me swing him. He had Eric's hair and eyes, but his nose and mouth must resemble his mother.

We bought ice cream from a cart and while watching Everette in the sandbox, Eric talked about his past. "My Father and mother met in dental school and married before they graduated," he told me. "They had student loans to repay, and soon my sister, Jean, was born. Then nineteen months later, I came along." He went on, "Dad said they were very frugal. They took over a practice when Dr. Pierce retired." He went on, "They bought a large, older home and saved all they could. Jean and I had what we needed, but not many extras. Jean and I both worked as soon as we could."

"I married Karen Beck before I finished my journalism course at Junior College," he sighed and leaned back. "Everette was born and everything changed," he said, looking off in the distance.

I didn't say anything. He went on, "Karen didn't want to be a mother. She called her mother or sister often to come take the baby for a while." Eirc's head was hanging now, a wisp of blonde hair in his eyes, "I was already working at the paper and gone during the day. I never said a word to her about the messy house," he said. He sat back and sighed.

Another little boy had joined Everette in the sandbox. They would fill their buckets and make huge piles of sand, then knock them down, throw back their heads and laugh.

Eric went on with his story, "Mom and Dad retired early and moved to Key West. Jean married and moved out. She'd had enough of Karen's mess, watching her disrespect for our beloved home."

"One day, Karen's sister called me at work," Eric continued. "She said Karen left Everette with her without bringing his formula. I left work, took the formula, but decided I would just take the baby home." His voice was lower now as he said, "Karen came in around two in the morning, smelling of beer and cigarettes, wearing tight jeans and a tube top. As calmly as I could, I told her to go to bed and I'd take care of the baby. The next morning, I got up early, left a note and money on the bathroom vanity." It read, 'Take your stuff and find somewhere to go. I have the baby. See you in court.' I took Everette to my sister and saw a lawyer friend of mine. And here we are."

I said, "I'm sorry, Eric." There was nothing else to be said.

Eric suddenly stood up, looked at his watch and said, "If I'm late getting him home, I'll never hear the end of it." He gathered Everette and his bucket, buckled him in his car seat and asked, "Do you mind if I take him home first?"

Karen was at the door when we drove up. When she saw me, her face changed …. if looks could kill.

We did something together every weekend, noth-ing special, just a movie or eat and drive around, playing music and talking. Eric always gave me a goodnight kiss … nothing special either.

Everette's fourth birthday was on October twenty eight. Eric bought him a spider-man costume for Hallow-een which would be on Eric's Sunday to have him. Karen invited Eric to the party at Chucky Cheese and made it clear not to bring "that woman."

On Halloween, we took Everette out early to a cou-ple of subdivisions where other parents were with their little ones. Everette was amazed at all the candy and kept taking it out of his bag, saying "I don't like these, or oh, boy. This is my favorite."

We got him home on time and went to Casey's Deli for a light supper.

Eric had been acting kinda giddy all day. He slid into the booth with me, put his arm around me and said, "I've got a treat for us at the house, a nice bottle of wine. Are you interested?"

I said, "OK, but I can't stay long. I have work tomorrow."

As we entered the house, it was almost dark, only one dim light on. Eric led me to a huge sectional sofa and said, "Get comfortable, Honey, I'll get the wine." I slipped off my shoes and curled up. He came back with two glass-es of chilled red wine. He handed me one, walked across the room and turned on the music, Lionel Richie's, 'All Night Long'. He sat close and we sipped the wine, neither speaking. The song replayed.

Suddenly he sat his glass down, put a hand under my hair and cupped the back of my head, pulling me to him. He kissed me, soft and sweet. I kissed him back. He pulled my shirt over my head as I unbuttoned his. He leaned me back and made gentle love to me.

We were now exclusive ... I thought.

I was really busy through November. I worked, studied hard, and the days flew by.

Karen started calling Eric with emergencies. "Everette needs a bigger bed now. Will you buy him one and put it up? Everette has an ear ache and wants you to read to him tonight. My car has a flat tire, can you come?"

Thanksgiving was one week away, and I realized I had barely seen Eric all month. I asked if we were having Thanksgiving together.

I thought his ears turned a little red. He said, "I promised I'd eat with Everette. He's been making turkeys at pre-school. He just now knows kind of what it means," He looked to see how I was taking it.

I covered it up pretty well, "Oh, It's fine. The girls at Mrs. Daniels invited me."

So that's what happened. Mrs. Daniels, Robin, Phyllis and I went to the Country Kitchen and stuffed 'till we could barely stand up. Most of the other women had family to go home to.

December was busy. My semester was coming to an end. I had always been a fast learner and was making good grades. My professor, Mr. Harris, asked if I would be interested in tutoring three or four students two times a week for one hour. He said, " The pay is really good, Faye, if you have the time."

"Oh yes, thank you, Mr. Harris, I'd love to."

Actually, I really needed the money. I was saving all I could. I had not bought any new clothes or an extra thing since I came to Cloverdale.

The old Monte Carlo was just hanging on, and I wanted to trade up as soon as possible.

I shopped for Eric and Everette wondering why Eric hadn't mentioned anything about what he might get me.

Mrs. Daniels put a big, beautiful tree in the lobby and hung a stocking on the mantle for each of us. I reckon the girl with the black eyes had gone back to him after he promised never again?

Don and Penny gave me a two hundred dollar bonus, which I took directly to the bank.

I had planned to spend Christmas Day with Eric after he dropped off Everette's gifts.

Mrs. Daniels had planned a movie night, pajama party on Christmas Eve with eggnog, pie and cookies for what few of us that were still here for Christmas.

On the way home on Christmas Eve, I picked up a box of chocolates for Mrs. Daniels and a bag of mixed hard candy for each of the others.

Mrs. Daniels met me as I entered the lobby. She seemed to have a drawn look on her face. She held out an envelope and said, "Your young man left this for you."

I guess I had a drawn look too. *What in the world was this?* I thanked her and hurried upstairs, ripped open the envelope and could hardly believe my eyes. It read, "Faye, this is one of the hardest things I've ever had to do. The last few months Everette has been begging me to come live with him. He sees kids at preschool with mommies and daddies. Karen explained to me that she had postpartum depression. We are gonna give it another try. You deserve the best. I will never forget you. Have a great life." Eric.

I fell back on the bed, a little numb, but really not shocked. After all, It was not a great romance as we had neither ever said the 'L' word. *He was not even man enough to tell me face to face. I guess I dodged a bullet,* I thought.

Why do I feel so light? I thought. I tore the letter into tiny pieces and flushed it. I showered, put on my best pajamas, tied a red ribbon in my black hair and went down to the party. The movie was *It's a Wonderful Life*. We all knew it by heart, but ate, drank eggnog, cried a little and had a great time.

After Christmas break, I got down to business at school. I registered for two other classes that I needed to be a teacher's assistant. *One day, I'll be a teacher,* I told myself. Tuesday night and Thursday night I tutored three or four students in Social Studies. I was really saving money now.

I never bought papers anymore. I didn't want to see "that" face. I was really okay. Eric didn't come into the steakhouse anymore. Don nor Penny said a word. I'm sure they knew why.

I now had a best friend in my class. Cindy Carroll was getting a degree in early childhood development. We hit it off right away. Cindy is a petite blond, blue eyes, even a turned up nose.

She and her husband, Drew, had bought a home on the White Tail River. I went to Drew's birthday cook-out and met several neighbors, mostly young couples with children.

Drew worked for the railroad and was gone sometimes for two or three days. Cindy said, "I feel totally safe, the neighbors are all friends. "

I knew then, "I'm in the right place."

When the semester was about over, I looked at my bank balance. "Wow," I said. "I've really done great. I can probably get a little trade-in on the Monte-Carlo."

I had asked Drew to help me with my car shopping. "I don't trust myself," I told him. "I don't want some used-car salesman taking advantage of me."

Drew and Cindy picked me up on Sunday afternoon. Drew said, "Most of the dealerships are in a one mile area north of town. They call it 'Swindlers Row'." He threw back his head and roared with laughter.

Drew looks huge next to Cindy, so opposite, with almost black hair and brown eyes, his arms muscled and big hands.

All the car lots were closed. We strolled around, peeping in windows, looking at price stickers on windows. Drew made comments about each one I seemed interested in. "Too much, Faye" or "Mileage too high, Faye."

My heart almost skipped a beat when I spotted a red Nissan Rogue on the Hollister Nissan lot. I had wanted one since the first one I had ever seen. It always parked next to me at the casino. I was almost screaming, "Look Cindy, isn't it perfect?"

While I looked for scratches, Drew kicked tires, opened the hood, checked the oil, and mumbled to himself.

Cindy was excited, "Oh, look at the interior, Faye, it's like brand new." The interior was beautiful beige seats, beige leather trimmed the doors and dash.

"Oh, Cindy," I squealed. "I'm afraid to hope!" Drew put down the hood, walked around some more, and looked at the price again. I was holding my breath, waiting for what he thought. He said, "Sweet ride, Faye. I hope you get it."

I screamed and hugged him around the waist, then Cindy joined in and we all did a little happy dance. I said, "Let's not get my hopes up too high. I don't have it yet."

The next morning, I called Don and told him about the car. "Sure, Faye. Take your time. We can handle Monday and good luck, Honey."

I had already cleaned out the Monte-Carlo, and been through the car wash. This was as good as it was gonna look. It was a hot, muggy morning. I pulled a pair of bright yellow shorts and a white tank top from a drawer, brushed my hair back and put a yellow headband on it.

As I slipped on beaded sandals and checked myself in the mirror, I thought, *I hope I'm not too casual to conduct business.*

CHAPTER THREE

Zach Hollister grew up in Cloverdale. He had an older brother, Phil. Their parents were George and Sarah. George was Pastor of Cloverdale Community Church. Sarah was a hospice nurse and an organist at the church.

Zach and Phil had a rather strict, but fair upbringing. Both played sports in high school, dated with parents permission, and worked odd jobs. They both attended two years of community college just to please their father, who really wanted at least one of them to attend seminary.

They took general business courses, really just passing time because it had already been discussed in private with their uncle Paul that they would take over his Nissan Dealership after proper training. Uncle Paul had been there over thirty years and only wanted an overseer job.

Phil married three years ago and their baby girl was due soon. Zach had never been really serious about anyone.

This particular Monday morning, Zach and Phil were standing around in the showroom, watching for a potential customer on this humid morning when an older model Monte-Carlo pulled up. A vision in yellow shorts and shiny black hair crawled out. It was as though a sunbeam shined directly on her.

Zach didn't know what hit him. "This one's mine, Phil," he said as he tried to stroll out casually. He felt like his tongue was stuck to the roof of his mouth.

She had gone to the red Nissan Rogue and was looking inside. "You're a real beauty," he blurted out, caught himself and said, "She's a real beauty, isn't she? I'm Zach Hollister." He put his hand out.

Faye was hesitant. After all, he was a car salesman and this was the first (big) thing she had done on her own. But she had practiced what she would say. She shook his hand and asked, "What's the story on this Rouge?"

Zach gulped and said, "It's a program car."

"I don't know what that means," Faye told him.

"Oh, it was a rental for two years, real low mileage, just like new."

"May I try it out?" she asked.

Zach was beside himself. "I'll go get a key and we'll go for a ride."

As he practically ran to the office, Phil caught up with him and said, "Zach, are you okay? You're sweating and red-faced."

Zach unexpectedly heard himself say, "Never better – that's the woman I'm going to marry!" Zach thought, almost out loud, *Faye Hollister.*

He went over all the features of the Rogue and Faye got in the driver's seat. Zach told her to take it on the highway and "See what it'll do."

Faye was loving it more when she saw all the dash controls. "Are you married, Ms. Dobbs?" he asked.

Faye laughed and said, "I don't have time, I'm in college and work at Don's Steakhouse."

God, she smells good, he thought. *We'll have to make some time. What in the world has come over me?*

Zach said, "I haven't been to Don's in a good while. I'll have to drop in."

Faye glanced at him and smiled. He really was good looking, with dark brown hair and green eyes. She said, "I'll be glad to wait on you."

They went into the office to talk figures. Her heart sank. She was gonna be a little short on cash. Faye stood up and said, "Thanks, Mr. Hollister, but I don't think I can swing it."

She turned to leave and Zach practically jumped over the desk. *She can't leave,* he was thinking.

"Ms. Dobbs, my uncle, who owns this dealership, is in Atlanta at a dealership convention. I'll call him later today and see if we can't do business."

Faye's face changed. "Do you really think so, Mr. Hollister?"

"I can almost guarantee it," Zach answered. "Give me your phone number and please, call me Zach."

"Okay, Zach, and you can call me Faye." She offered her hand and thanked him. Zach had never felt such a soft hand. He looked at it. Long fingers and beautiful nails. He realized he had not let go when she tugged away.

I'm making a fool of myself, he thought. "I'll phone as soon as I hear something," he said, thinking, *Don't let her leave, Zach.* But she drove away in the old Monte Carlo, and he watched her until she was out of sight.

Phil was watching it all from the showroom. Zach came in and plopped down in a chair. He was weak and shaky. Phil said, "Bro, I've never seen you so shook up. Want coffee or something?"

"A coffee won't cure this, Phil. I've been hit by a thunderbolt and don't know what to do."

Phil said, "Same as always, Zach. Ask her out and get to know her."

Phil was the manager and approved all sales. Zach showed the figures on the Rogue. "We can't go that low, Zach. Uncle Paul would have a stroke."

Zach paced the showroom and finally said, "What if I give up my commission, Phil?"

"What? Wow, boy, you've got a bad case. If that is what you want, okay with me."

Faye's phone rang at eight-thirty that night. She had just taken off her shoes and laid across the bed. It had been a really long day, last week of school.

She saw the name of her caller, Zach Hollister. She was almost afraid to answer, afraid of disappointing news.

Faye had told Cindy what went on. Cindy said, "I know a little about that family. Mrs. Hollister was the hospice nurse who took care of my grandmother."

"Hello, Zach," she answered. "What's the verdict? Are you making me the happiest girl in Cloverdale?"

Zach took a second to answer. "I have every intention of doing just that," he finally breathed out. "When can I see you, uh, I mean when do you want to close?"

"I'll be there about nine in the morning, if that's okay. I don't need to lose any more work now that I'm broke."

"Fine, Faye. See you at nine. Good night."

"Thanks, Zach. Good night."

Faye called Cindy and Drew with the news. Cindy said, "Drew said you need to latch onto Zach Hollister. He's a catch."

Faye laughed. "I haven't had much luck in that department."

Zach took extra time with his grooming. He had not fallen asleep until late, still seeing that yellow vision standing by the red Rogue, still smelling that perfume. He tried to be professional and not make any mistakes. It went very well. As he handed Faye the keys, he had a sinking feeling that he would never see her again.

As she turned to leave, he called out, "Faye, what's the lunch special at Don's today?"

Faye smiled and said, "Mushroom steak with gravy and peach cobbler ala mode."

"See you at about twelve thirty," he said.

Faye smelled the still new of the car. She could hardly believe she had really done it. "Shows you can do lots if you put your mind to it," she said aloud.

Zach was thinking, *Boy, you can do anything if you put your mind to it.* Zach was there on time and asked for Faye's table.

They talked briefly as she poured his sweet tea. "Yes, the car is great."

Faye was busy through lunch. Zach lingered. When Faye brought his check, he said, "Faye, I won't beat around the bush. Will you go out with me? I have references."

Faye looked into those earnest, green eyes and without hesitation, said, "Call me later."

That was the beginning of a once in a lifetime romance. Zach took Faye to church the next Sunday. He was so anxious to have his parents and friends meet her. Faye loved Reverend George and Sarah right away.

After the service, several people, young and old, welcomed Faye and invited her back. It was a good day. Sarah invited Faye to dinner later in the week. Faye thanked her and asked, "What can I bring?"

"Just your sweet self and smile. You have a spell on our son."

The weather was really warm. Zach and Faye spent every moment they could together. Zach would break out singing:

YOU ARE MY SUNSHINE,
MY ONLY SUNSHINE.
YOU MAKE ME HAPPY
WHEN SKIES ARE GRAY.
YOU'LL NEVER KNOW DEAR
HOW MUCH I LOVE YOU.
PLEASE DON'T TAKE MY SUNSHINE AWAY.

Zach and Drew became instant friends. Drew took Zach fishing in his little boat and showed Zach how to grill the perfect burger.

Faye realized she was absolutely, hopelessly, head over heels in love when she found herself thinking of Zach if she woke in the night and first thing every morning. As for Zach, he called her the moment he was up. He had to hear her voice, and the sight of her made a pain in his gut.

Faye was still working at Don's Steakhouse. She would be at Hollister Nissan when Zach quit each day. Sometimes they would get some supper. Sometimes,

Faye would have snacks and drinks in the Rogue, and they would go to the park and sit in the gazebo, holding hands and talking about their childhood.

Zach was completely speechless when he heard Faye's life story. He put his arm around her, wiped a tear from her cheek with his knuckle and kissed her. It was a sweet kiss and short. Zach said, "Sorry Faye. Did you mind?"

Faye looked at the sorrow in his eyes, turned her face up and kissed HIM. They looked at one another and laughed.

They really liked going to Cindy and Drew's. They all went swimming in the river several times. Just sitting on the dock watching the sunset, close, with their arms around one another, heads leaned together, just the sound of their breathing.

One Sunday afternoon, Zach and Faye were picking up Drew and Cindy for a movie. As they turned on Windmill Lane, Faye saw a 'For Sale' sign on the second house on the right. "Oh no," she squealed. "Why would anyone leave here?" Faye asked Cindy the same question.

"A widow lived there," she said. "She went to an assisted living facility. Her son is selling it. I heard it needs some remodeling."

They took Cindy and Drew home after the movie and dinner. As they went back up the street, Zach suddenly pulled into the driveway of the vacant house. "We'll have some privacy here and watch the moon come up." They cuddled and kissed for a long time. Zach never went further than that. He told Faye, "My dad preaches abstinence."

The moon came up bright, shining on the white blooms of three huge Crepe Myrtle trees, its reflection on the river. Zach whispered in her ear, "Darling, I love you so much."

"Zach, I love you more.," Faye whispered back. Faye had never been happier.

The next Saturday, Zach told Faye he was taking off work early and would she meet him at the gazebo?

Faye had been waiting for several minutes wondering, *What's keeping Zach?* She finally saw his pick-up turn in. Zach got out, opened the back door and fumbled around. Faye said to herself, *What in the world is he doing?*

Zach was holding something behind his back with both hands, grinning from ear to ear. "Close your eyes, Honey, and hold out both palms."

Faye said, "You'd better not scare me." Then she felt something warm and fuzzy and squirming. She opened her eyes. It was absolutely the sweetest, cutest, big-eyed puppy she had ever seen.

"Oh Zach, he's so precious. Where did you get him?" She was getting kisses from the puppy now.

"Well, to begin with, he's a she and I got her at the shelter. Her mama had nine babies and there is no room for her," Zach told her. "Do you want her?"

"I'd love to, Zach, but Mrs. Daniels doesn't allow pets."

Zach said, "That's OK, Honey. I'll keep her for you. What will you name her?"

"I'll call her Angel," Faye said, "'cause that's what she is."

Zach had a serious look come over his face, and he said, "Take that yellow ribbon from her neck." As Faye was untying it, Zach was going down on one knee. When Faye pulled off the ribbon, something fell on her bench. She picked it up and gasped. It was a ring.

"What's this?" she whispered.

"Will you marry me, Faye Hawkeye Dobbs?"

Faye almost threw the puppy straight up. "Oh yes, Zach, nothing would make me happier."

Zach pulled her against him, almost crushing the puppy. He put the ring on her finger. They kissed and Zach realized he was crying. He stood back and looked at Faye. She was too.

Phil's wife Lynne, delivered baby girl, Joy, on June second, and her christening was that Sunday. Zach had told Phil about his surprise proposal. Sunday after the christening, Phil said in a loud voice, "Folks, this isn't the only thing we have to celebrate." Everyone looked at him. "It's my pleasure to announce that my little brother is getting married."

Everyone cheered and shook hands. "Congratulations! Best of luck," came from the crowd.

"When's the big day?" Zach's dad asked.

Zach looked at Faye. She was pale and speechless. "What about July twentieth, Honey?"

All Faye could do was nod her head.

"Oh my," Sarah Hollister said. "There's so much to do. I'll help you Faye. Of course, it'll be held here, and George will perform the ceremony, and I'll provide the music."

Time flew by.

Don and Penny bought Faye's dress for a gift. Cindy gave her a shower. Mrs. Daniels, girls from the rooming house, Penny and Suzanne from the restaurant, and a few neighbor women Faye was acquainted with attended.

Faye was overwhelmed. She would have almost everything she needed.

Zach told Phil about the house on the river. Phil picked up his phone, called the Realtor, and got all the information. "Zach," he said. "It's not over priced, but I know how much you make here." He went on, "I don't think you can make the down payment."

Zach was thinking of Faye looking in the windows, loving that house. She had never had a real home.

As Zach and Faye were leaving church the next Sunday, Zach's dad stopped them. "Hold up kids," he said. "If you don't have plans, I'd like to take you for a drive." Zach and Faye looked at one another, puzzled. Neither one would refuse this strange request.

When his dad turned on Windmill Lane, Zach gasped. "Dad, where are we going?"

George was turning into the house, "Right here," he said.

The Realtor was on the porch, the 'For Sale' sign lying beside her. Faye was so weak in the knees, she could barely stand.

"What is going on, Zach?" she whispered.

His dad explained, "Let's look around, and if you really love it, your mom and I will make the down payment for your wedding gift."

Faye couldn't help but hug him. Tears in her eyes, she followed the Realtor through the house, leaning heavily on Zach. It needed some work, but it could be perfect.

A large living room with a gas fireplace, a dining room and a large kitchen (she would redo the cabinets), three bedrooms and two baths. "It's just perfect," Faye squealed. And just like that, the house was theirs.

There was never a more glorious day for a wedding. And never a more beautiful bride. As Faye walked down the aisle on Don's arm, carrying a bouquet of yellow Calla Lilies, sun shone on her from the skylight. Zach watched her with a lump in his throat. *I was right,* he thought. *She is a ray of sunshine.* As they were pronounced man and wife, they looked into each others' wet eyes and knew they would be in love forever.

After the reception, Zach and Faye ran from the church in a shower of rice, laughter and shouts as she threw the bouquet. Mrs. Daniels caught it and roared with laughter.

Zach and Faye had talked about how much they would love to honeymoon in Hawaii, but in the end they fixed up the house instead. They would honeymoon later. So no one knew they were going to their new home for their wedding night.

Faye went to freshen up in their master bath. When she came into the bedroom, Zach was standing in the middle of the floor. When he saw her, his heart was racing. He walked to her and took both her hands in his, stepped back and looked from her head to toe. "Just let me take in all your beauty," he said. He pulled her long, silky hair over her shoulders and ran his finger around her ear and down her neck.

Faye felt a shiver go over her.

Zach kissed her long and deep.

Without saying a word, Faye took him by the hand and led him to their bed.

CHAPTER FOUR

Zach and Faye, and sometimes Cindy and Drew, spent the month of August painting the walls and cabinets, replacing tiles in the bathrooms and changing locks. Faye put the new key on her keyring. Zach slipped his into his pocket. They were so surprised when the old carpet came up and revealed beautiful hardwood floors. Faye did a happy dance and got busy refinishing all those floors.

Zach trimmed shrubs, planted some roses for Faye and made sure the fence was safe for Angel. They fell asleep in each other's arms every night.

Two weeks before school started, Faye got the call she had been praying for. She was accepted as full-time substitute teacher at Cloverdale Middle School.

Don and Penny almost cried when Faye gave a two weeks notice. They were almost like parents to her. Zach went with her to break the news to them. Don said, "Well, at least have a bowl of peach cobbler on the house. In fact, I think I'll have one too."

Fall went by quickly it seemed...

In no time, Zach had the fireplace turned on in the evenings. He and Faye snuggled under a blanket, watching TV or talking about their childhood. They planned out their future as though it were a sure thing. They would wait three years to start a family. They would have two sons and one daughter, who would look just like Faye.

The holidays were wonderful.

Zach's parents insisted on hosting every occasion. Faye didn't argue. She wasn't much of a cook, but she was learning.

They decided to save money for their future honeymoon and only bought a larger bed for Angel and placed it near the fireplace. Angel was at a big-footed, awkward age, all over the place. Her favorite game was chasing cardinals from the bird-feeder.

In early spring, Zach brought home a fishing magazine someone had left in the customer lounge. He was engrossed in it when Faye came in from shopping. "Hey, Honey," he called, "come look at this fish. It was caught not too far from here." Faye stopped and looked at the picture.

"Yeah," she said, "but he's fishing from a boat."

"Sure would be nice," Zach mumbled. "I could teach you how to fish."

"Honey, those boats cost thousands," Faye reminded him.

"I know," Zach replied. "I'm just dreaming, guess I have spring fever."

Every time Faye looked around, it seemed he had that magazine. She heard Zach on the phone with Drew,. He had been by a boat dealership: Zach hadn't said a word about it to Faye.

In April, the annual sales for the previous year were reported at Hollister Nissan. Zach was the top salesman for the entire eastern district. Uncle Paul, Phil, and the entire crew at Hollister Nissan catered a dinner for Zach after closing on that Friday. Uncle Paul stood up, cleared his throat, and made a little speech about his nephews. He then called Zach to come stand beside him. Paul put his arm around Zach and congratulated him and handed him a check. Zach was speechless. He looked at the check and turned white. It was for twenty thousand dollars. Zach backed against a chair and sat down.

"Faye," He croaked, "we can have our honeymoon."

Faye was elated, Zach worked so hard He deserved a vacation, but Faye had something else in mind.

The next Sunday afternoon, Faye said, "Let's go for a drive, it's so beautiful out. I'll take you in my Rogue and we'll get ice cream."

Zach rolled off the couch, dropping the magazine on the floor. "Sounds good," he said, as he pulled her to him and kissed her.

Faye drove directly to the boat sales.

Zach looked at her and said, "What's this about?"

Faye turned to him and took his hand. "Darling," she said, "we can always go to Hawaii, even if we're old." Zach started to protest, Faye put a finger over his lips. "No, listen to me, Zach," she went on, "You work so hard, and a boat is something we can enjoy for years."

"Well," Zach said, "it won't hurt to look."

A used bass boat caught Zach's eye. It was a metallic blue, eighteen footer. The price was right. Zach looked it over from stem to stern. Faye enjoyed watching him, like a kid in a toy store.

On Wednesday afternoon, Zach took off work early and hurried to the boat sales lot.

She was still there, gleaming in the sun.

Bill, the salesman, went over everything with Zach. "You got to get her registered, Zach. You can do that on-line. " Bill went on, "What's her name? I'll get it put on for you."

Zach didn't hesitate, "Hawkeye," he said, "In big yellow letters."

"You can pick her up Friday afternoon," Bill said. "I'll clean her up and she'll be ready to sail."

That Friday afternoon, Zach and Faye were both absolutely giddy with excitement.

'A FISHING WE WILL GO'

'A FISHING WE WILL GO'

'HI-HO, THE MERRY OH'

'A FISHING WE WILL GO'

Zach was singing so loudly, Faye joined in. In no time they had the "Hawkeye" hooked behind the pick-up and were on the road. A new sushi bar had opened in town.

Faye said, "Let's celebrate and try the new place." Zach was so happy, he would agree to anything. He parked and opened her door.

He picked up Faye and swung her around, "Tomorrow, I'll teach you to fish, baby." They ate a big meal, sushi, pork quoza and topped it off with key lime pie. Faye and Zach were both groaning, "I'm so full, I don't think I'll eat for a week." Zach moaned, rubbing his belly.

Zach got his fishing gear stowed in the boat. Faye brought towels, sunscreen and old hats. She got out a cooler and filled it with power drinks and ice, added a container with two cold cut sandwiches. After all, they wouldn't be gone all day.

They were exhausted by bedtime, still not wanting a snack tonight. They showered together, made love and fell fitfully to sleep. The alarm was set for six. At about two, Zach jumped out of bed and ran to the bathroom. He had the trots. A few minutes later, Faye was in the other bathroom. After about an hour and a dose of medicine, they drifted back off to sleep. Zach shut off the alarm and started to just stay in bed.

But, he told himself, "I'll be OK when I throw some water on my face." Zach shook Faye's shoulder. "It's time to rise, Sunshine."

Faye didn't even turn over. "Honey," she said, "I just can't make it this time. You go on and catch a big one for me."

Zach sat on the side of the bed. Something told him to lay back down with Faye. *But the 'Hawkeye' is waiting and it's a gorgeous day, I'll just go out for a while,* Zach thought to himself.

He kissed Faye on the forehead, never dreaming it would be the last time for years. "Get some rest, my darling. See you later." Another stop at the bathroom, and Zach was gone.

CHAPTER FIVE

Zach put in the boat at the Oak Grove Boat Ramp about seven. He put his wallet, wedding band, and phone in the glove box. *'Hawkeye' is a beauty*, he thought to himself. *I'll see that Faye gets our honeymoon in Hawaii before too long. I'll outsell everyone again this year.*

He trolled down to a spot where he and Drew had caught a few. He caught a small bass and threw it back. The sun was beginning to really beat down on his head. The movement of the water and heat were making him dizzy. Zach thought, *I hope I don't have an accident on the boat.* He laid his rod down, put the motor in neutral, reached for one of the old hats and collapsed.

A short while later a boat was coming from the opposite direction. Two young men were in it, one driving and one standing straddle legged with his bait skimming the top of the water. He spotted the 'Hawkeye'. He couldn't see anyone on the boat. He called out, "Hey, anyone on board?" Then he said, "Hey, Dwayne, I don't think anyone's on this boat? We'd better see what's going on."

Dewayne pulled up to the "Hawkeye" and stood up to look. "Bo, there's a body in there. If I get you steady, can you jump on it and see what's going on?"

"Sure, bro, no problem," Bo assured him.

Dewayne did a good job, not scraping the boats.

Bo jumped on board, landing with his knees on Zach's legs.

"I think he's dead, Dewayne," Bo called out.

"Well, nit-wit, check his pulse." Dewayne said.

Bo turned Zach over and could see he was barely breathing. "He's still alive, Dewayne, but not by much. What'll we do?"

"Let me think, Jug-head, let me think." Dewayne was quiet for a minute, looking up and down the river. Not a boat in sight, it was too hot for fishing now. He lowered his voice and asked, "Are you still itching for a boat?"

Bo looked up, his eyes big, "What you talking about, Dewayne?"

"Well, how much gas is in that tank, Bo?"

"I'll look bro." Bo quickly looked at the body, then the gas gauge. "It's full Dewayne. Why?"

"Here's what I'm thinking. In a few hours, we can be near Careyville. You cover him with towels." He went on with his plan. "If he wakes up strong, we'll say we're taking him to a doctor. If he doesn't wake up, we'll unload him where he can be found."

"I'm skeered, Dewayne," Bo was visibly shaken.

"Okay, chicken," Dewayne replied. "Do you want that boat or not? All you gotta do is paint a new name on it."

Bo mumbled, "Yeah, I want it. Let's go."

"Here, catch this." Dewayne was pitching a heavy flash light to Bo. "If you have to use this, make it count," he told Bo.

They looked up and down the river again, got their stories straight and headed down river. It was late afternoon. They only saw two boats, nothing to concern them.

They had gotten about thirty miles when Zach moaned and tried to sit up. Bo picked up the flash light, stood over Zach and delivered two hard blows near Zach's temple. Blood was everywhere, Zach couldn't move. He looked dead for sure.

"Oh God," Bo called. "Dewayne, I killed him. What'll I do?"

"Cover him up and get on with our plan," Dwayne called back. Dewayne pulled his phone from his pocket and made a quick call. It was their sister who answered.

"Sis," Dewayne said. "This is very important. Bring Daddy's truck and boat trailer to Five Points Dock about dark and don't be late or say anything about it."

"Okay, but it's going to cost you," she replied.

They had traveled roughly eighty miles with Dewayne looking for a good place to stop. He finally saw a dark slough and motioned for Bo to follow him. He pulled in, cut the motor off and dropped the anchor.

Speaking in little more than a whisper, he guided Bo to do the same. They listened for any voices or noise. Not a sound.

Dewayne crawled onto 'Hawkeye' and uncovered the body. They didn't take time to see if he was alive or dead. It was all the two of them could do to pull the body to the edge and roll it up on its side.

"Go on three, Bo." Dewayne counted. They gave a big grunt and the body slipped into the water. They sneaked away like the rats they were.

CHAPTER SIX

Faye finally got out of bed about nine-thirty. Angel had to go out, so Faye, her stomach rumbling, made it to the patio door. She was weak, but managed to make a cup of ginger tea. She sank into a dining chair and sipped the tea. *Wonder how the fishing is going?* she thought. *I expect Zach home by three. It'll be too hot for the fish to bite by then.*

Faye was forming a girl's soccer team at school. She had to be there by five this afternoon. "Gives me some time to rest," she said aloud. She let Angel in and fed her, then headed to the couch. She was asleep in just a few minutes.

When Faye woke, it was eleven o'clock. She felt a little better and decided to call Zach. The call went to voicemail, "Hey, Honey. Hope you're having good luck. Remember you're going with me, for soccer tryouts at five. Love ya, bye."

Faye tried to reach Zach several times in the next few hours, but no luck.

She was beginning to worry. "What could be wrong? Maybe he dropped his phone?"

Every time a vehicle came down the street, she jumped up, expecting to see Zach, grinning at her, waving. About four, Faye called Drew. "Have you heard from

Zach?" Drew had not. She called Phil and Zach's dad. No one had heard from him. Everyone was getting concerned now.

Faye called her assistant coach and told him she couldn't make it for tryouts.

She called Cindy. "Cindy, will you ride to the Oak Grove boat ramp with me? I'm worried Zach's had trouble with the new boat."

Drew followed in his pick-up. He was also worried. Zach was not very experienced with boats.

At the boat ramp was Zach's pick-up with the boat trailer. A fisherman was loading his boat onto his trailer. Drew went down to talk to him. "Have you seen a metallic blue bass boat, the 'Hawkeye' out today?"

The man shook his head, "Nope, I've been out since about noon, nothing biting." He continued, "I've been several miles in both directions. Sign's aint good today." He spat out a stream of tobacco juice and went about his business.

Meanwhile, Faye was calling the sheriff. Within thirty minutes, search and rescue were there. Drownings were not that unusual around here. When they learned who was missing, they really got busy. This was Reverend Hollister's youngest son.

Soon the water rescue boat was launched. Faye was about to have a breakdown. Cindy hugged her. "They will find him, Honey. His boat probably ran out of gas or broke down." It didn't comfort Faye. As dark came she was crying and shaking.

She realized suddenly, she had not eaten all day. She said, "Cindy, do you have any candy or anything? Zach and I were sick last night and I haven't eaten." Cindy went to Drew's truck and brought back a box of Moon Pies. One of the officers brought them bottles of water.

It was over an hour after dark when the search team gathered back to the ramp. They had searched both banks of the river. The sheriff talked to Faye. "Mrs. Hollister, we've done all we can till daylight." He took her hand and looked in her red, swollen eyes. "You go home and try to rest. We'll put out a call for volunteers in the morning."

Faye nodded her head, but she knew she was not leaving here without her husband. Everyone was gone when Faye turned to Cindy and Drew. "Cindy, will you take care of Angel? Zach might come in yet and I'll be here."

Cindy knew not to argue. She would do the same thing if it were Drew.

Faye ate another Moon Pie, curled up in the back seat, made sure the doors were locked and surprisingly fell asleep. Sleep didn't last very long.

The moon came up bright on the water. Night sounds were all around her. It was not yet dawn when Faye got out of the Rogue and stepped behind a tree to pee. She just got back in the car when people started arriving. Before long there were at least sixty searchers wearing boots and gloves, making a plan where to search. Four boats launched and went in different directions.

Zach's parents missed church and brought Faye coffee and a sausage biscuit. They hugged Faye and prayed for Zach. Zach's brother, Phil, was one of the searchers.

The day wore on with no news. Faye barely knew what day it was. Night fell again with no luck. The sheriff sat down on the ground by Faye. It was a difficult conversation to have. He had said it to many families before.

"Mrs. Hollister, I don't like to tell you this, but tomorrow we will start recovery efforts."

Faye sprang up, "NO! You can't give up! Zach's alive, I can feel it!"

"Go home, Mrs. Hollister. You're exhausted and there's nothing more you can do."

But Faye didn't go home. She stayed awake as long as she could, watching for Zach.

The next day, they dragged the river for miles with no result. Faye felt as though she were two people. "What in the world has happened?" she cried.

Phil finally convinced her to let him take her home. The house was so dark and quiet until Angel saw her and licked her all over. Faye fell into a chair and petted Angel. "Sweet Angel, I'm glad you don't know what's happened." She made herself take a shower and shampoo her hair and just in time. People were dropping in with food and flowers, trying to console Faye, offering any help she needed.

Faye felt as though she were floating, just barely acknowledging what was going on around her. Everyone was finally gone, except Stephanie and Kellye, twin sisters from church, who insisted on staying the night with her. Faye was glad they did, she wasn't capable of being alone.

The girls actually stayed three nights, driving Faye to make arrangements for a memorial service for Zach.

Faye felt as though she had a hole through her that anyone could see through. She could barely find words to express herself. Thankfully, the family helped her take care of all the things that needed to be done. Faye never knew there were so many legal things. She barely remembered the service … it seemed she was in a fog.

After a couple of weeks, people stopped coming by or calling so often, except of course, Cindy and Drew. Whatever would she do without them?

By the last of May, Faye got back to working with her soccer team. She had lost weight and was pushing herself everyday and crying herself to sleep every night. Zach's pillow had the smell of his cologne and she hugged it to her until the smell was gone.

The day of their first anniversary, Faye was really depressed. Cindy and Drew invited her to dinner, but she begged off. She put in a movie, 'Ghost', with Demi Moore and Patrick Swayze. She couldn't have made a worse choice. She cried herself to sleep on the couch, hugging Zach's old pillow.

Summer passed and Faye went back to teaching and studying for her teaching certificate. She attended most games at school, never missed a PTA meeting, keeping herself busy.

Cindy and Drew had a big, beautiful baby boy. They named him Easton. Faye babysat as often as she could get her hands on Easton, with a pain in her heart.

The years went slowly by.

CHAPTER SEVEN

The first thing I remember, I was on all fours, puking my guts out. My head was splitting. I put my hand to my left temple and brought it back covered in blood. I wiped it on my sleeve and rolled onto my side.

Nothing looked familiar. The only sound was the river below me and the tweeting of a bird not too far away. I must have dozed off again, so I opened my eyes. The sun had moved far west. I was able to sit up and waited for the dizziness to go away. I thought I heard a vehicle on the other side of this bank. I half crawled and half stumbled up the rise. It seemed to take forever. I thought, *How can I be so weak? What happened to me?*

I finally crawled up to a two-lane country road, but not a car in sight. I sat down where anyone could see me and hoped for a ride before dark. Several cars and trucks passed me by, avoiding looking at me. *Who would stop for a bloodied man in the middle of nowhere?* I thought. I wiped more blood off my face and laid back down.

I heard the sound of an old truck, slowing down. Before I could sit completely up, I saw an old pair of work boots walking towards me. I tried to stand, but couldn't.

The man looked about seventy-five years old, skinny with twinkling blue eyes. He was wearing faded jeans and an old uniform shirt buttoned at the wrist. He was stronger than he looked, he grabbed me under my arms and got me steady. He said, "Hey Sonny, what does the other feller look like?"

I said, "I must have fallen and hit my head. I'm dizzy and can't think straight. Where are we?" I asked.

He answered, "We are in Carey County. Where are you headed?" He went on, "I can give you a lift for a few miles if you don't mind riding in the back with Nanny." He went on, "Me and the little woman have been to a 4-H show and bought a prize nanny goat."

He had her tied in the bed of his pick-up. He stuck out his hand, "I'm Leonard Johnson," he said and nodded toward the truck where a gray-haired, round-faced woman sat. "This is my wife Grace. I call her Gracie."

I offered my hand and said, "I'm….uh….I'm…. uh… I'm, my GOD, I can't remember my name. I must have hit my head harder than I thought. Guess I better get it looked at."

Leonard said, "Ain't no place open 'til Monday. You'd best come home with us and rest awhile."

I didn't argue. I realized I was in a predicament. With his help, I crawled into the bed of the truck. About that time, Nanny let loose and peed, splattering all over my tennis shoes. Leonard laughed, and I tried to, but it hurt my head too much.

We had not gone more than two miles of pot holes until the smell of the diesel got to me, I banged on the truck and Leonard pulled over. I leaned over the tailgate and puked 'til nothing was left but dry heaves. I fell back in the truck, not caring about goat pee.

Leonard brought a piece of sherpa from the cab and tucked it under my head. I never knew when the truck started again. When I roused, the moon was high and the truck was turning into a gravel road. I sat up and turned around to see where we were.

A porch light was on a small white house. Leonard pulled right to the porch to help me out. Grace hurried to open the door and turn on the lights.

It was slow going up the three steps and into the house. Leonard helped me to an old couch, took off my shoes and threw them on the porch. He said, "Just stay still 'til I get Nanny settled." He went on, "I gotta get her fed and watered."

Grace hurried to the kitchen and came back with a bottle of nausea medicine. It was almost empty, she said, "Just turn it up and get all of it."

I didn't hesitate, I think I would have tried anything. Grace brought a cold, wet cloth and put it on my throat and it felt so good. Grace was a pretty woman, a little on the plump side with beautiful hazel eyes. She reminded me of Mrs. Santa.

Leonard came into the kitchen and went to wash up then came into the living room.

"How are you feeling, Sonny?" he grinned, "You look like hell warmed over." He chuckled, "I reckon you'll make it, a young feller like you."

He turned on an old radio that was sitting on top of an old TV. "TV's been out for awhile," he said, "I don't really miss it, but the little woman misses her shows." He leaned his recliner back and hollered, "Gracie, make me a pimento cheese sandwich."

She called back from somewhere in the rear of the house, "Make it yourself, old man, I'm busy."

Leonard groaned, got up and went to make his sandwich.

Gracie came in and sat beside me. I could tell she had been crying. She pointed to a picture of a young Marine on the mantle and said, "That's our son, Robert. He was killed in Afghanistan." She wiped tears away. I looked at the picture – Leonard made over. She went on, "You're in no shape to go anywhere, you're spending the night here." Her voice cracking now, "I fixed Robert's bed and laid out some of his clothes. They may be a little big."

I didn't know what to say. I wasn't in any condition to argue. "Thank you, Grace," was all I could get out.

Grace went on, "When you feel up to it, you can get a shower and I'll make you some dry toast."

I did as she said. After all, I didn't know who or where I was. I could be a killer or a robber, but these were trusting, God fearing old people.

Leonard helped me to the bathroom. As soon as I saw the toilet, I really had to go. I turned on the water, took off the filthy clothes and once again went through my pockets. Nothing in them but a single key. I stared at it, rubbed it and stared again, trying to remember something, but nothing.

I stood shakily in the shower, it felt so good, but I knew my strength was running out. I had to hurry. I was washing my arms when I saw a small butterfly tattoo on my left forearm. *Maybe that's a clue to who I am,* I thought.

Grace had laid out a complete set of clothes, even socks. I managed to pull on the jeans and shirt, but couldn't button it. I carried the socks and made it down the hall. I could hear Leonard and Grace in a whispered conversation. I knew it was about me. I had to figure out something, someone to call, somewhere to go, but nothing came to me.

I got to the couch and sat down with a plop. A sad look came over Leonard when he saw me in his son's clothes. The clothes were a little big, but not much.

Leonard watched as I sank back on the couch, holding the socks. He took them from my hand and pulled them on me, saying, "Well, Sonny, you sure smell better." He grinned; he had a great smile.

Grace came in carrying a glass of ginger ale and a slice of dry toast, saying, "Try to get this all down. You must get hydrated."

I did as I was told; it was actually good. I said, "Thank you all so much. I don't know when or what I last ate."

I sipped the cold ginger ale and could feel it cooling my insides. I finished it and realized it was really quite good. Leonard had turned off the radio and was asleep in the recliner, Grace in her rocker, we were all about asleep.

Suddenly Leonard stood up and said, "Well, I think it's about bedtime."

Grace, startled, pushed herself up. Leonard offered to help me but after giving myself a minute to clear my head, I followed him down the hall to a small bedroom with a lamp lit beside the bed. The covers were turned back. Nothing ever looked more inviting.

I sat down on the bed, glanced around and said, "I can't thank y'all enough Mr. Johnson. I'll get out of your hair tomorrow."

He said, "Call me Leonard, Sonny, and we'll see what tomorrow looks like Good night." He closed the door behind him.

The bed was firm and smelled so wonderful. I took the key out of the jeans and looked at it again. "I can't remember," I mumbled.

I didn't know when my head hit the pillow.

When Leonard knocked, then opened the door, I was already half awake. He asked, "How'd ya rest, Sonny? Feel like eating some breakfast?" The smell of sausage and coffee wafted down the hall.

I sat up and rubbed my eyes. "Good morning, Leonard. Yeah, I think I could do with a little breakfast."

He said, "Well, wash up and come along."

I washed my face and hands, squeezed some toothpaste on my finger and rubbed my teeth and gargled, looking at myself in the mirror. *Who are you? Is anyone looking for you?,* I wondered. I wet my hair and more or less put it in place with my fingers. I looked at the cut on my head. *I'll have a scar for sure,* I thought.

I followed the smell to the kitchen. It was nineteen seventies, but clean and large. Grace had the food on the table, two plates of sausage, eggs and hot biscuits. Butter and a pint jar of homemade blackberry jelly sat in the middle of the table, and at the other seat was a cereal bowl of soft rice and a slice of dry toast.

Grace sat down a glass of cold ginger ale and said, "You'll be able to eat real food soon."

Leonard blessed the food. Their steaming cups of coffee smelled familiar. *Maybe I'm a coffee drinker?* I wondered. I actually enjoyed the light breakfast. I was feeling much better.

Grace said, "I have your clothes and shoes in the washer. You can get your own clothes on if you want."

She was clearing off the table.

Leonard said, "Let's go on the back porch, Sonny. I think I'll puff my pipe a little before I feed the stock."

The porch was screened with a few cushioned chairs. Leonard had an old table beside his chair with his pipe and cherry tobacco. The aroma of the tobacco was sweet.

Am I a smoker? I wondered.

I looked around the yard. It was about two acres, all fenced, a small barn and a chicken coop with a fenced run. About eight hens, at least two with chicks were scratching and clucking around. One red rooster strutting around. To the left of the yard was a beautiful vegetable garden with beans strung on twine and cages around the tomatoes.

The sun was shining at one end of the porch. A calico cat was stretched out in it. Grace came onto the porch carrying my wet shoes and sat them in the sun, saying, "Move over Calli Cat, you're hogging the sunshine."

Just then Leonard went out to feed and water Nanny, the chickens, and a rescued burro he called 'Ol Jack'. He let the screen door slam behind him.

"That ol' man will never learn to hold that door." Grace said as she sat down, took off her glasses and wiped her eyes with her apron. She went on, "We go to church most Sundays."

I said, "I'm sorry I've messed up your plans. If I can get a ride to the nearest town tomorrow, I'll probably get this straightened out," I went on. "So this is Sunday, huh?"

She said, "Yep, Sunday, April twenty-six."

"No wonder it feels so great out today." I replied.

They both sat quietly, watching Leonard getting Nanny acquainted with 'Ol Jack. The pair seemed to hit it off as 'Ol Jack started running and kicked up his heels.

They talked about the weather. Leonard lit his pipe again, and the morning passed. Grace went in to fix a little lunch and soon called, "Ya'll get in here. It's ready."

They had pimento cheese sandwiches. They looked delicious and sweet tea. Grace had thin chicken soup, crackers, lemon jello and the rest of the ginger ale for me. Suddenly I was overcome with emotion.

I said, almost choking up, "I can never repay you folks. Leonard, if you'll take me to see a doctor tomorrow, I think he can fix me up and this nightmare will be over."

Leonard answered, "Sure thing, Sonny, we'll go into Careyville to the clinic." I asked him how far to Careyville. He said, "About fifteen miles." We moved to the front porch, out of the sun after lunch.

Leonard put some records on his old phonograph, George Jones, Marty Robbins, Don Williams and Tony Bennett for Grace. I didn't know any of the singers. Leonard told me about each one. He had a beat-up old guitar leaned against the wall and picked it up and strummed along.

We walked around and looked at the garden, just getting a good start. I loved the smell of the soil. *Maybe I'm a farmer*, I thought.

Grace said, "I'm going in and start some supper," she looked at me and continued, "and since you're doing so well, I might surprise you."

I watched as Leonard took care of the stock and gathered eggs.

Grace did surprise me with a bowl of delicious chicken and dumplings. I bragged to her, "Grace, I'm sure I've never tasted anything this good." Then she brought out a lemon loaf cake. I said, "If I don't get out of here soon, I'll have these jeans filled out."

The evening passed with Leonard telling stories of thirty-nine years working in a chair factory in Careyville.

Grace had retired from the high school where she was a cafeteria lady.

Leonard had some music playing, and we were all quiet, it had been a long day.

When the music stopped, Leonard rose slowly from the recliner, stretched his arms above his head and yawned, "I guess we should turn in; gotta get up early and get to Careyville," he said. We all said goodnight.

I thanked them and went to Robert's room. I hadn't looked around the room this morning, so I turned on the ceiling light. Apparently it had not been touched. High school banners, trophies, pictures of Robert in his football uniform and his high school year book. His clothes were still in the closet.

I turned out the light and went right to sleep, somehow feeling at home.

The next morning, we were having an April shower. After a breakfast of biscuits and sausage gravy – I did like coffee – Leonard and I ducked our heads and ran to the truck. On the way, I looked out the window for anything familiar. It was beautiful farmland, pastures of cattle, silos, barns, churches and houses.

I asked Leonard, "Does Careyville have a police department?"

He answered, "Sheriff Owen will be there. We'll talk to him."

In no time it seemed, we pulled into Careyville Health Clinic. We were second in line to see Dr. Steve Nolan, M.D. The doctor was about my age. I hoped to myself that he knows what he's doing. I told him my story. I don't think he had ever encountered an amnesia patient.

Dr. Nolan shined a light in my eyes, held up three fingers and asked, "How many fingers do you see?"

"Three," I answered.

He felt the lump on my head and called the nurse who had taken my vital signs, "Louise, please clean this cut. I'm gonna put a couple of stitches in it." He looked at me saying, "I need to check something." Louise cleaned it with something that really stung.

Dr. Nolan returned, and as he pulled in the stitches, he said, "Amnesia is a strange thing. Some will recover their memory in time. Some will recover all at once, and some people never will."

"Thanks Doc," I said. He hadn't given me much hope.

Dr. Nolan gave me a prescription for my vertigo, told me to rest for two weeks and, "Come back if you need me."

Leonard stopped at a drugstore to fill my prescription. He bought me a toothbrush, razors, and a comb. I saw some free calendars on the counter and took one. Leonard paid and said, "We're going to the sheriff's office now, Sonny."

Sheriff Owen Stewart was a big man. He and Leonard met with back slaps and "How's it going?" Leonard pointed to me and said, "Owen, this young man needs some help. Can we talk in private?"

"Follow me." The sheriff showed us into a small office with a gold badge painted on the door. We took seats in front of a huge mahogany desk. The sheriff sank into his swivel chair, looked me over and asked, "Okay, young man, what's going on?"

I told him everything I knew with Leonard helping me. "Do you know of any missing men?" I asked him hopefully.

He blew out a big sigh, leaned forward and thumbed through some papers on his desk. He called in his booming voice to his desk sergeant, "Hey Henry, get on that computer of yours and check for any good-looking young men that might be missing."

He chuckled and said, "Well, young man, we can print a 'John Doe - Have you seen me?' poster and get it out."

Leonard stood up quickly, walked to the window and looked out. Without turning around, he said, "Not 'John Doe.'" He turned and looked me in the eye, "How 'bout Bob Johnson, Sonny, 'til we get news from your family?" He went on, "We gotta call you something to get you to supper."

I was startled, but they were both laughing. Suddenly, I was laughing too. "I guess that's as good as any," I said. And Bob Johnson was born.

Leonard drove me around Careyville, the usual brick courthouse in the heart of town, small cafe's, two law offices, a shoe store, jewelry store and other small shops. He drove west of town a couple of miles and showed me the chair factory where he had worked for thirty nine years. The factory parking lot had hundreds of cars.

"I didn't know it was this huge," I said surprised.

"Oh yeah," Leonard answered, "We ship chairs, recliners and sofas all over the United States. It's a great place to work."

As we headed back, Leonard pulled into the gas station and filled up. The rain had stopped and the clouds were moving out. Next stop was a fast food drive-thru. We ate while driving. Leonard dropped mustard on his shirt and Bob Johnson hooted with laughter.

May the third, the mail carrier brought two social security checks about ten-thirty. We were all ready for a shopping trip to Careyville. Grace had a long list and I wanted to help Leonard with some repairs around the place. I recovered enough to do 'something'. Leonard was anxious to get started while he had 'Bob' to help.

I almost felt like a kid as I climbed into the bed of the pickup and we set out. We finished shopping around three and Leonard took us to Annie's Cafe for fried catfish and hush puppies.

We had so much in the truck, Grace had to squeeze in the middle. We were all tired and happy. Suddenly Leonard broke out singing.

> 'NOW OLD DAN TUCKER WAS A FINE OLD MAN,
> HE WASHED HIS FACE IN A FRYING PAN.
> COMBED HIS HAIR WITH A WAGON WHEEL,
> DIED WITH A TOOTHACHE IN HIS HEEL.
> NOW GET OUTTA THE WAY OLD DAN TUCKER,
> YOU'RE TOO LATE TO GET YOUR SUPPER.
> SUPPER'S OVER AND BREAKFAST IS COOKING,
> OLD DAN TUCKER JUST STOOD THERE LOOKIN'.

It was new to me and I roared with laughter. By the time we unloaded groceries, lumber, fencing and animal feed we were about spent. Leonard and I collapsed on the porch. Grace had put away the groceries.

Now she came out carrying a tray with three bowls of peach cobbler with ice cream on the side. As I ate, I thought, *This has been a good day for "Bob Johnson."*

Then suddenly, a sad, melancholy feeling swept over me. *What's wrong with me?* I thought.

I offered to leave several times over the next couple of months. It would upset Grace the most. She would beg me to stay a little longer. "Just until you get some news, " she would say.

I called Sheriff Owen every Monday.

I read the local paper, looking for anything familiar.

Leonard and I fixed the roof on the chicken coop, mended sagging fences for 'Ol Jack and Nanny, who were best friends now, built new steps for the back porch, mended the screen door and put a modern faucet on the kitchen sink for Grace.

The garden was in, we picked beans, sat on the porch and snapped them while Leonard and Grace told stories of the 'good old days'. Grace put the beans in the freezer, made bread and butter pickles and canned tomatoes.

Summer was flying by. One evening Leonard asked Bob, "Do you fish, Bob?"

I answered, "I don't remember. Why?"

Leonard said, "I thought we might get the old flat bottom out and try our luck tomorrow."

"Sounds like a good trip." I was excited.

The next morning we got the chores done fast and hooked up the boat and trailer. Leonard put in rods and his tackle box.

We were all set when Grace came out with lunch, saying, "You two would starve if I didn't feed you."

Leonard put in at his favorite place and trolled upstream talking all the time. He had Robert on his mind and started telling me all about him. I sat quietly and let him get it out.

Robert was their only child, born late in life. He was a standout football player, an ROTC member and scholar. Robert and Nicole Cox were sweethearts all through high school and married the summer after graduation. They moved in with Leonard and Grace, who loved it.

Robert talked to his dad and told him, "I can't spend my life making chairs." He shocked Leonard when he blurted out, "Dad, I've joined the Marines. I'm training to be a diesel mechanic. Nicole agrees with my decision."

Grace took it so hard, Leonard thought she would collapse.

Nicole was already expecting and moved back to her parents.

After boot camp, Robert was sent to Afghanistan. He was killed in a barrage of bombs three months and nine days later.

Leonard paused, his voice breaking, "We almost lost our minds," he went on. "NIcole had a baby girl, named her Hope. She has Robert's blue eyes. For a couple of years, we got to see Hope often," Leonard went on, "Then Nicole remarried and moved away. It broke our hearts."

So they both retired, telling themselves they would travel, something they had never done. But it never happened. They saw a TV show about rescue burros and drove three hundred miles and brought 'Ol Jack home, settled into a routine and took care of one another.

Suddenly, Leonard looked around and said, "Goodness, I've yakked so much, I went too far. Let's cast out here then head back down river."

"Do you have a top water plug?" I asked without thinking.

"A what?" Leonard had a surprised look, "You are a fisherman, how else would you know about a top water plug?"

"I don't know," I answered as I put the plug on.

In just a few minutes, I had a good bite. I worked it in, laughing at Leonard trying to get his net ready. It was a big bass. "Looks like supper, Pop," I said, not noticing that I had called him Pop.

But he noticed and grinned from ear to ear. "Here, Son, let me net him?" I held the fish up. It was full of eggs. I had to let her go. As I leaned over the side to watch her swim away, something came over me. I was nauseous and dizzy.

We didn't have any luck and Grace laughed at us.

That night I dreamed of a house by the river and a blue boat.

The next day was Grace's quilting bee at church.

Bernice, the neighbor, picked her up. Every other week they had a few friends from church gathered to quilt, gossip, sing hymns, laugh and sometimes cry over someone's loss. They took turns keeping the quilts or giving to someone in need.

As soon as Grace left, Leonard said, "Hey Son, come out to the barn with me, there's something I want you to see."

I said "Sure," and followed him to a stall with a lock on it. Leonard swung open the door, reached in and pulled a tarp off something and threw it on the ground. I was really surprised when he rolled out a brand-new motorcycle.

"Wow!" was all I could say.

"This was Robert's graduation present." Leonard was about to cry. He went on, "He loved it, but didn't get to ride much, so I want you to have it. It's a Yamaha Venture," Leonard said. Tears were now streaming down his face.

I was overwhelmed, "Pop, I couldn't."

"But I want to know who has it," he croaked. "But, of course, I have to clear it with Gracie."

We both sat down in the hall of the barn, staring at the bike, neither speaking. I realized we were both sniffling a little.

Leonard cleared his throat and blew his nose. "Son," he said, "I won't take no for an answer. Gracie and I are no spring chickens, my blood pressure and arthritis, and I know you've noticed Gracie isn't as sharp. I had to turn the stove off yesterday. It was red hot."

"But, I don't know if I can even ride," I half whispered.

"Well," he said, "Let's run down to the auto store, and we'll get a new battery, plugs and some new gas. You'll be on it before dark." And that's exactly how it happened. Leonard was bubbly as we got the bike started. He rode it out of the barn.

"Here, Son, get on." He then asked, "Can you drive a car?"

It struck me hard, " I have no idea," I answered. I was so nervous as he showed me how everything worked, even more as I straddled the seat.

Leonard handed me Robert's helmet, black and gold, his school colors. "Just go slow around the yard," Leonard told me, "Watch out for trees and above all, Gracie's flowers."

I gave a little gas and wobbling every which way, finally got it balanced and made it around the house without doing too much damage.

He slapped me on the back and said, "You're a natural, Son. Tomorrow, I'll drive behind you and we'll go down the road."

After a couple of days, it felt like I had been riding for years. After I did so well on the bike, Leonard suggested I drive the pickup. I was anxious to find out if I had ever driven. To my amazement, I was an excellent driver.

Everyone in Careyville seemed to know my story.

I called the sheriff, "Sheriff Stewart, do you think you could help me get a driver license?"

"Come on in," he answered. "We'll see what we can do; we'll figure out something."

I was able to get a temporary one after I was finger-printed and my picture made. That evening we were all on the front porch. I had something on my mind, so I said it. "I want to get a job and pay you back somehow."

Leonard sat up and excitedly said, "Son, that's a great idea. Would you like to try the chair factory?" He went on,

"They pay well. Gus Wicke is the head honcho. We can go see him tomorrow."

I said, "I'd like to give it a try."

Leonard picked up the old guitar and started singing:

YOU ARE MY SUNSHINE,
MY ONLY SUNSHINE.
YOU MAKE ME HAPPY,
WHEN SKIES ARE GRAY.
YOU'LL NEVER KNOW DEAR,
HOW MUCH I LOVE YOU,
PLEASE DON'T TAKE MY SUNSHINE AWAY.

Suddenly, I thought I was going to start crying. I went off the end of the porch and out to the corral. 'Ol Jack came up to get his head rubbed. "I don't know what came over me old boy." I told him.

I had put "The Key" under the table lamp. It was the only clue to who I am and I couldn't lose it. That night I took it out, rubbed it, stared at it, even smelled it. It just smelled like brass.

I dreamed of a house by a river and a beautiful dark-haired woman.

CHAPTER EIGHT

Leonard introduced me to Gus Wicke at the chair factory. He said, "I can really use you if Barbara in H.R. can get you a permit."

Barbara Stewart was the sheriff's maiden sister. She knew my story well. "I think I can take care of this, Bob." She started pecking on her computer and handed me an I.D. and permit. I started to work the next day.

I drove the truck on my first pay-day. I had things to bring home. A TV for all of us, a microwave for Grace, new boots and clothes for me. But most of all, a wallet with a slot for "The Key."

I hugged Grace when I gave her the microwave and said, "You'll love this, Mom." It was the first time I called her Mom. She had tears in her eyes. I wiped them away with my knuckles.

On my second payday, I asked Gus if I could leave an hour early. He said, "If you finish that stack of frames." I got busy and clocked out seventy minutes early. I had important things to do.

First, I bought myself a phone. Next stop was the local paper, *Careyville Banner*. A nice young man came to help me. I said, "I would like to put an ad in the three largest newspapers in the state." I explained my circumstances. The photographer took a good picture of me. The ad was simple. Just my picture and the message… "Do you know me? Very Important! Call 335-884-4328."

I felt lighter going home. Now I will hear something. Leonard and Grace were glad to hear that I was making an effort to move forward.

I didn't hear anything the first week. I caught myself constantly looking at my phone. After three weeks, I ran ads again, this time for the Sunday editions.

When I didn't hear anything, I began to feel a little despondent. Leonard and Grace tried to keep me encouraged. I would be okay one day, and not want to get out of bed the next. One good thing, I was making friends at work.

One Friday, Josh, who worked with me said, "Hey, Bob, some of us are gonna shoot a little pool when we get off. Wanna go?"

I stuttered for a second then answered, "Sure thing. Maybe that's just what I need."

We were just like cowboys at the end of the trail, strutting into C.J.'s Pub and Pool Room, glad our week was over and money in our pockets.

Josh ordered a round of beer and got us a table. All the pool tables were busy. I didn't even know if I could play. I took a sip of beer – what a strange taste. The second drink was better, somehow refreshing. We finally got a pool table and I found I could play a little, but couldn't win a game.

Before I realized it, the sun had gone down. I had been here for over three hours. I said "So long" to the guys, finished my fourth beer and headed home. Slowly.

Leonard came onto the porch to meet me, saying, "We were worried. Are you okay. Why didn't you call?"

I stepped up on the porch, grabbed Leonard and danced him around laughing, "I'm fine and dandy, Dad, fine and dandy."

Leonard pulled away from me and said, "You're drunk, boy." He pushed me to the door. "Get in the bathroom and wash your face and use some mouthwash. We'll try to keep Gracie from knowing. I'll talk to you tomorrow."

I stumbled over the threshold as Gracie called from the kitchen, "I'm warming your supper."

I called back, "Thanks, Mom. I ate in town. I'm so tired out, I'm gonna hit the hay." I avoided Leonard's eyes and made it down the hall to my room, closed the door, collapsed on the bed staring at the ceiling.

I was exhilarated, thinking of the fun of being with people my age. The music, the laughter, the lights, people dancing. I never had such fun. "I'm going again, whether Leonard likes it or not."

I fell asleep and dreamed of a big, golden dog chasing me. Leonard woke me around ten o'clock with a cup of coffee. "I lied to Gracie for you, boy." He looked me in the eye, "I told her you worked over."

I sat up, took a big slurp of coffee, cleared my throat and told Leonard of my evening. Leonard took a big breath and sat down by me on the bed. He stared at his feet, not saying a word for a couple of minutes.

Finally, he spoke. "Bob," he paused again. "I'm going to say this as plain as I can." He sounded kinda choked up and didn't look at me. He continued, "Gracie and me have come to think of you as our own." He paused and cleared his throat. "I can't begin to know how you feel, not knowing who you are, and especially why no one seems to be looking for you. I do understand why you need friends your own age." He looked at me and grinned. "I was a young whipper snapper once." He went on. "Gracie changed me, got me in church and settled me down." He stood up and said, "Now we're gonna talk to Gracie. That is after you get cleaned up and eat something." He walked out without looking back.

I looked in the mirror. I didn't look quite as rough as I felt. I got a shower and shave, ate a bowl of cheerios and joined Leonard and Gracie on the back porch.

Callie Cat jumped on my lap, purring her big purr. It was calming to stroke her. Leonard knocked the ashes from his pipe and said, "Bob, I've told Gracie the truth. She understands that you need friends. We don't expect you to spend all your spare time with two old geezers like us."

Gracie put in her two cents worth, "Speak for yourself, one old geezer." That brought a laugh that broke the tension.

Leonard said, "We discussed asking you to move out, but we both agreed that wouldn't be good for any of us. We believe that it's just a matter of time before your family finds you." He stood over me and laid down the law.

"First thing," he said sternly, "Let us know if you'll be late. Second, don't drive drunk, even if you sleep in your truck. It just ain't worth it."

He took his keys from his pocket and took his house key from the ring. "Here's my key, boy, just don't wake us up when you come in late." Leonard grinned and slapped me on the back. "Now let's get the chores done."

I felt like crying. They could not be more loving if I was their son. Did I ever have parents of my own? Was I an orphan? Did I have children somewhere? I was really low as we took care of the stock. Afterwards, I went to my room, took "The Key" from my wallet and rubbed it, saying, "Give me a clue, Key, tell me something."

I had a headache. I put my dirty clothes in the washer and laid down. Leonard and Grace were going into town. I fell asleep and had a bad dream. The house by the river was drifting away, the big golden dog was chasing it.

It was early afternoon when I woke up. The headache had eased. I have had them often since my accident, whatever that was. I put my clothes in the dryer, made a peanut butter sandwich, heated a cup of coffee and went to the front porch. I watched the birds as I ate, then suddenly I laughed out loud. I was thinking of the guys I was with last night. Josh, of course, Derek, he and Josh are both married and didn't cut up much, but Bubba, yes, he looks just like his name. Bubba is the life of the party, with his shirt tail hanging out over his big belly. The girls love to tease Bubba and all will dance with him.

I decided I would go to C.J.'s again, make friends and maybe get over the blues I've had lately. Someone may even recognize me. I don't want to give up on that.

I went into the house and marked another day off my calendar. There were a lot of X's now. I heard the truck pull in and went to help unload the groceries. Leonard and Gracie looked tired and grim. I know they must have been talking about me.

I told Leonard, "Relax. I'll help Mom put away everything."

"Thanks," he said. He fixed himself some coffee and headed to the porch.

"Go on to the porch, Mom. I'll finish this." I told her.

She looked at me and said, "You're a good boy." She got a glass of iced tea, changed her shoes and went out to rest. The tea looked so good, I got myself a glass and joined them.

They were both quiet, just staring at the yard. After a few minutes, I spoke. "I'd like to talk to y'all about me staying here." Leonard's rocker came to a sudden stop. "I don't think it's fair for me to take advantage of you any longer." Neither of them said a word. I went on. "I'm making good money and can afford to move out."

I heard Grace gasp, but I continued, "Or if you want me, I can pay room and board and help around here. Next month, I'll have enough to pay down on a truck."

Leonard and Grace didn't have to look at each other after nearly sixty years together. Grace was the one who did the talking this time. "Of course, you'll stay with us as long as you want." She looked at me. She was crying. "You know how we feel about you."

"It's settled then," I said. "Just tell me how much, and I'll start paying today."

Leonard spoke up, "Wait until you get your truck and see what your payments are."

"Sounds good to me," I said. "I'll go put the stock up. It looks like a storm coming up."

"Thanks, Son. I'm going to watch the news." Leonard was slow getting up. Then he helped Grace up to go inside with him.

Grace called back to me as I headed to the barn. "We ate in town. There's left over meatloaf in the fridge."

"Thanks Mom," I called back, but the wind blew my words away.

Ol' Jack and Nanny were already at the barn door. I swung it open and they hurried in. The chickens were at roost, talking low to one another.

A huge lightning streak, followed immediately by nearby thunder, sent me dashing to the back porch. I scooped Calli Cat from a chair cushion and shut and locked the screen door. I put her down by her bowl of food and took my clothes from the dryer and into my room to hang up. Rain was pouring now, the old tin roof drowning out everything. I laid down and watched the lightning flash outside the window. We were really having a good rainstorm.

Suddenly, I felt so alone, like I wanted to cry. "Who am I?" I said out loud. "Where did I come from?" Once again, I took "The Key" from my wallet and stared at it. *Maybe it doesn't mean anything,* I thought. "Or maybe, it means everything," I mumbled. I went into the living room to see the news with Leonard.

Without looking at me, he said, "Son, the world is going to hell in a hand-basket."

"I know," was all I said.

Grace came in with her robe on and curlers in her hair. She was getting ready for church tomorrow. Leonard stood and stretched and said, "This is putting me to sleep. Think I'll get a shower and go to bed early."

Grace said, "Okay, Honey. I'm looking at my Sunday School lesson and I'll be right behind you."

I had been reading a James Bond novel. I picked it up and turned the TV off. We couldn't hear it anyway. *Wow*, I thought, *If I had some of Bond's gadgets, maybe I could learn my identity.* I had a solemn spell come over me and closed the book.

Sunday, while the folks were at church, I had an urge to work. Maybe to pay penance for Friday night? I put on my old worn out shoes and went to the barn. I took a big rake and cleaned the chicken house out. Then I moved a load of manure from Ol' Jack and Nanny's stalls. Usually Leonard kept them clean, but I had noticed he was slowing down.

The air outside was fresh after the rain. I decided to get cleaned up and ride the motorcycle down the country road for awhile. It was a two-laned, asphalt road. Just a few houses, mostly hayfields. I rode for several miles, really just trying to clear my head. I decided to head back and take care of the stock for Leonard.

My mind was drifting. Suddenly, I had a thought. *If I drive into a tree, my problems are no more.* I looked at the speedometer, I was going over ninety miles an hour.

Thankfully, there were no trees along there. I slowed and tried to clear my mind. Surely the rest of my life can't be this? There must be a life for me somewhere.

The folks were home. I drove the bike into the barn and noticed my hands were shaking. My heart was racing too. *Guess I'm spending too much time alone, stressing over who or 'what' am I?*

I stepped up on the side of the porch. Leonard looked at me with a worried look. "Bob, what's wrong, Son? You're pale as a ghost and shaking like a leaf."

I fell into a chair and told half-truth. "I got up too much speed on the bike and scared myself," I told him.

"It can get away from you in a hurry," he said.

Grace called us for an early supper and we spent a quiet evening.

Two weeks later was the folks' sixtieth anniversary. Their Sunday School class had lunch and a party after services. I went with them. Everybody looked so old. *I've got to get acquainted with someone my own age,* I thought as we rode home.

I marked off the calendar each day. No one was looking for me. I had the dream of the house and river. Sometimes I felt like giving up, but I decided it was anxiety and I'll fight it.

I didn't go out with the guys for several weeks, although I always heard what a great time they had. I was saving for my truck. When I had a good down payment Leonard took me to Careyville. It was so exciting. We looked at several trucks, and drove some of them. Leonard was almost as excited as I was.

I bought a black Ford crew cab with low miles. It drove like a dream. We were both excited to show Grace. I went in the driveway blowing the horn, Leonard right behind me blowing his. Grace was excited for me, kissed my cheek, saying, "I made a special supper for my two men."

I felt happy and excited as a kid with a new toy. I wiped every speck of dust off the truck. I couldn't wait for Monday to show the guys. They all had trucks. At lunch break, a crowd came out, all bragging about what a great deal I made.

That Friday, Josh asked me to 'C.J's' again. "It's karaoke night, Bob. Jane, my wife, is gonna take home the prize."

The place was packed when I got there. I spotted Bubba alone at a far table, got a couple of beers and joined him. Josh and Derek had their wives with them at another table. They got up to dance once in a while. The music was so loud, we couldn't carry on a conversation.

After about an hour, Bubba said, "Let's go outside for a while and get some fresh air." I pushed back my chair and was a little unsteady. The air did feel good after all the smoke inside. Bubba said, "I've got some good weed, wanna light a joint?"

I had to think, *What is he talking about?* I'd heard some of the guys talking about it. "Sure," I said. Little did I know that the few steps to his truck were my first path to hell.

CHAPTER NINE

I admitted to Bubba, "I don't think I've ever done this." Bubba showed me how and we sat in his truck with the windows down, and I began to feel so relaxed, better than I'd ever felt – at least that I could remember. "What will this do to me?" I asked.

"Oh, nothing bad," Bubba answered. "It may make you a little dizzy, but it doesn't last long. And," he added, "it makes me hungry, but it's worth it for the feeling I get." He looked at me. "Without a little weed, I would never have the courage to ask a girl to dance – I know how I look."

I was really feeling loose now and my headache was gone. "Where do you get this?" I asked Bubba.

"I've got a connection. Do you want some?" he looked at me seriously. "It will be twenty bucks."

"How often should I smoke?" I asked.

"Whenever you feel uptight or just need to relax." Bubba stuck out his hand, and I laid a twenty dollar bill in it.

CHAPTER TEN

Winter and the holidays were coming up fast. I wrapped all the water pipes and went with Leonard to a neighboring farm and bought a truck load of hay for Ol' Jack and Nanny.

Grace cooked a wonderful Thanksgiving meal. We watched TV all day. Parade in the morning and football the rest of the day. I was surprised that Grace knew so much about it, also that I knew so much.

I was smoking a joint every time my head started pounding. After a few weeks, it didn't help.

The factory closed for Christmas week. We went shopping and bought each other little gifts. I went to see the Christmas play at church. It's title was *A Christmas Miracle.*

"I'm the one who needs a miracle." I was wallowing in self pity for sure.

Now I was taking "The Key" from my wallet every night before I turned out the light. Almost every night, the dreams came, sometimes good and sometimes very bad. After the bad ones, I always woke up with a terrible, pounding headache.

During the week between Christmas and New Year, I went into Careyville to see Dr. Nolan at the clinic. Thankfully, he was there and remembered me. I told him about my headaches and the frequent dreams.

"I'm prescribing you a pain killer, Bob." He had a serious expression and looked me in the eye. "This can be addictive, only take it as needed and NEVER mix with alcohol."

"Thanks, Doc," I told him and shook his hand.

I filled the prescription, got a drink from the machine and swallowed my first Opioid. It took effect while I was driving home. I felt better and decided to smoke a joint, then put the windows down, so Leonard wouldn't smell it on me.

It was getting late when I pulled into the driveway. I was absolutely feeling no pain. I went straight to the barn to see if Leonard had put up the stock. He had not. I took care of them and entered the back door.

Grace was getting a wet cloth in the kitchen. She had a worried look and said, "Leonard almost passed out Bob. His heart is racing and his blood pressure is high."

"Do we need to get him to the hospital?" I asked.

He was laid completely back in his recliner, very pale. I could tell he was scared.

"Hey, Dad. You need a doctor?" I asked.

"I'll be alright in a while. I think I'm dehydrated," his weak voice answered as Grace laid the cloth on his head – her cure for most things.

He had been drinking lemonade. I sat him up a little and helped him finish it. We sat quiet for a while, listening to Leonard's shallow breathing. Finally, He asked for someone to turn on the news. We knew then, he was feeling a little better. But now I had a headache, went to the kitchen and took another pill.

I went to the barn on weekends to smoke my weed. They never noticed I was gone. I was late for work several times, especially on Mondays. I started going with the gang to C.J.'s every Friday and sometimes on Saturday also. I made friends with several regulars. Jane, Josh's wife taught me some dance steps, and I had the nerve to ask some of the girls to dance. It was a world I felt I had never known.

Occasionally, I would take one of the girls into the back seat of my truck and make out. I never had any romantic feelings for one of them. I wondered, *What's really wrong with me?*

I was taking my pills more than prescribed. The first time I ran out, I lied to Dr. Nolan and told him I had dropped them in the toilet.

He gave me a look that said, "I don't really believe you," but gave me another refill and a talking to. "Bob, I told you to be careful with how you take this." He added, "You only have one more refill. You may have to seek psychiatric help."

That kinda shook me. I must slow down with the pills. The next Saturday night, I was at C.J.'s until closing. I don't know how much I had to drink, but I left with a full one in my hand. I had smoked a joint with Bubba and was feeling no pain.

On the outskirts of town, I turned the can up to take a swig, swerved off the road and hit two huge trash cans. I didn't stop, I was scared to death that I'd be arrested for drunk driving. I had a lie ready when Leonard saw the fender. I told him one of the delivery trucks ran into it and would pay to fix it. I was getting to be a good liar.

The next Monday when I got to work, Gus was waiting for me. He took me out of hearing range of Josh. I just knew I was fired. Gus said, "Bob, you've been a good hand, but lately you've been late a lot and your production is slacking. Do you have an excuse?"

I pulled the pills from my pocket and said, "I've been having to see a doctor, Gus, you know my background, it's the headaches."

Gus paused for a minute. "I understand, Bob, but I'm responsible for production and everyone has to do their part."

"I'm getting better Gus, I can do my part," I assured him.

He slapped my back and said, "Good man," and walked away.

When I ran out of pills from Dr. Nolan, I panicked. It was taking more to help me now. I needed three or four a day instead of one. I went to a walk-in clinic and obtained a prescription with three refills. I was spending a lot for my weed, too. I knew I needed to slow down, but couldn't.

The nightmares came every night now. I was losing weight. I didn't get a haircut or shave.

CHAPTER ELEVEN

On Saturday night at C.J.'s, the guys were all dancing, so I went to sit at the bar. I had just sat down when a young woman slid onto the stool beside me.

She had bleached blonde hair hanging in her eyes, short shorts and western boots.

I had only just glanced at her when she moved closer and introduced herself. "I'm Carlie," she said, and flashed a big smile. "I see you in here all the time, but you never bring a girl?" she gave me a quizzical look.

"Well, Carlie, I'm Bob, and I haven't been here long." Carlie was chatty to say the least. I bought us a coupla rounds of beer. I don't know how many she'd had already. I know I was getting drunk.

She asked me to dance and we staggered around the floor with Carlie rubbing all over me. She guided me toward the door where it wasn't so noisy. "Do you have a car?" she asked.

"Well, I have a truck with a dented fender," I told her.

"Good," She said. "Let's go to my place, it's nearby and I have some really good stuff."

I looked at her and thought, *Why not?* "Sure, let's go. Just show me the way." Her place turned out to be down an alley three blocks away.

She told me to park on the street and we walked down a dark, dirty alley.

She stopped at a door and pulled me into a big room with a few candles burning. When my eyes adjusted, I could see old chairs and mattresses on the floor.

Four or five men and women were lying around in different stages of consciousness. Carlie guided me about half way down the wall to an old car back seat. She plopped down and motioned me to sit beside her.

"This is my pad," she said. "Get comfortable."

I watched as she felt behind the seat. She pulled out a small pouch, looked to see if anyone was watching… they weren't in any condition to know anything.

She took two pipes from the pouch and said, "You wanna smoke with me? It's great."

The condition I was already in had lowered any inhibitions I might have had. "Sure, set me up, Carlie," I told her and laid back on the seat. I didn't even ask what I was smoking… right then I didn't care.

I watched Carlie and did as she did. Soon I felt so big and strong. I could handle anything that came my way. Then I saw some flickering lights and closed my eyes. I don't know how long I had been there when I opened my eyes, looked around, and everyone was quiet.

Suddenly I saw a movement at the other end of the room. I squinted my eyes and lost my breath. The big golden dog was sneaking toward me. His eyes were bloody. Blood was running from his fangs.

I crawled toward the door. Just as I pushed it open he bit into my foot. I managed to drag him out the door,

I was screaming for help, but now he had my head in his mouth and was dragging me down the alley.

"Help me, somebody help me." I was crying.

The dog suddenly bit into my skull with all his strength. I heard, as well as felt, my brain explode. The pain was unbearable. I had brains in both my hands.

CHAPTER TWELVE

I could hear men talking. When I tried to sit up, I couldn't. I couldn't speak. I waited for a while and tried to raise my arm. I turned my head a little and squinted my eyes open. My wrist was chained to a hospital bed.

Suddenly a doctor was at my side, "Can you hear me, Mr. Johnson?" he asked as he reached for a chart at the foot of the bed. "You had a close call this morning. I'm Dr. Williams. I gave you something to help your craving," he said. "Do you need anything else right now? These gentlemen here need to talk with you when you can."

I croaked out, "I'm freezing."

"I'll have the nurse bring you some warm blankets and I'll see you later" Dr. Williams turned and left.

Suddenly, the sheriff was at my side. "I was sure surprised to see it was you my men brought in," he said. "Never woulda dreamed you were into hard drugs."

"I'm not," I croaked out. "An accident."

"Yeah, maybe," the sheriff looked as though he didn't believe me, saying, "Look Bob, I know your story, I know how you've tried to find your folks. I'm willing to cut you some slack if you want to get help." He motioned for someone who was sitting on the other side of the room.

Gus came to the bedside, put his hand on mine and squeezed it. He really had a hurt and concerned expression. He said, "Bob, you don't have to talk, just listen. The sheriff and I have discussed a lot while you were out. We agreed we have no idea what we would have done in your situation." He paused, then pulled up a chair and sat down.

"I've been good friends with Leonard Johnson for over forty years … Grace too. I know how they came to love you and I believe you love them." Gus's eyes grew moist. "You've been a good worker for me, so I've asked the Sheriff if he'll recommend you for this treatment center."

I was trying to understand what Gus was talking about. "My job?" I managed to say.

"I'll give you thirty days leave," he said. "You'll stay here and complete the program. The sheriff will not press charges if you don't repeat." Gus had it all figured out. "Your job will be waiting for you when you're well."

The sheriff interrupted, "I've had dealings with this center before with very good results. The therapist, Dr. Sherman, is the best."

Suddenly I had severe nausea and waved them out. "Yes, I'll do it." I called.

The sheriff turned back into the room, unlocked the handcuffs, patted my hand and said, "Good luck, son," and followed Gus out.

I closed my eyes and was about to doze when suddenly I was back in the alley. I felt to make sure my head was still there, I was so nauseous when a nurse came in with an IV pole.

"I'm going to get you an IV going," she said. "We want to get you hydrated." She worked quickly, found a good vein and had it going. "There's something in it to help with your nausea."

She checked my vital signs, turned out the light and closed the door. I watched the IV drip and was soon asleep.

I woke, needing to pee so badly and realized I already had. I panicked for a second, put my hand down my pajamas and felt. I had a *diaper* on!

Just then Dr. Williams walked back in, watching me pull my hand out of my pajamas. "I wet myself," I whispered.

"I'll send someone to help you," he said. "But first, I need to talk to you." He sat down and went on. "The sheriff said you want to enlist in our thirty-day program. I'll explain it briefly. Dr. Sherman is our therapist, one of the best in the state."

"You will be given one pill a day for seven days to control your cravings. I'll do all I can to help with the nausea and chills and other things you're gonna go through." He paused, "On the eighth day, you will receive an injection that will last for one month. That's when Dr. Sherman will start your therapy."

"Could I get something now?" I was begging him.

"No," he answered. "I gave you a pill after we got you in your room this morning. You'll get another tomorrow." He stood to leave, "I'll send someone to change you. You can't get up now." Soon a male nurse came and brought a dry wrap and put it between my legs.

"I'm freezing," I told him. "I can't feel my feet; they're numb."

"I think I can do something about that," he told me.

He returned with another warm, thick blanket and a heating pad, which he wrapped around my feet.

I went off to sleep after that, but soon a big bloodied dog was coming through the wall. I tried to get the sides of the bed down, screaming for help. The dog turned and was running down a long dark alley. I was right behind him. Occasionally, he would glance back at me with slobbers and blood flying from his mouth.

"Roll over Mr. Johnson," was all he could say.

I was so tired of running, I hurt all over. The alley was freezing cold and I was naked. Then I saw it … A steel cage at the end of the alley. The dog didn't see it. He ran into it and hit his head on the back of the cage. I had "The Key" in my hand and locked the cage, laughing at the dog, who was whimpering with his tail between his legs.

CHAPTER THIRTEEN

"Here, Mr. Johnson, try to take a sip," someone was putting a straw in my mouth. I got my eyes open and finally could see the nurse. I was in the hospital.

"What is it?" I asked.

"You've been very sick and unable to eat. This is beef broth. I thought you could take it best through this straw."

I sipped the broth, then felt myself peeing. "I'm wet," I told her.

"I know, Mr. Johnson. I'm coming back to clean you up and change your bed," she told me. "Dr. Williams wants to talk with you."

She came right back with a stack of sheets and wipes, saying "Roll over, Mr. Johnson." I shivered and almost jumped off the bed.

Dr. Williams smiled when he saw me with my head up on a pillow. "Well, well, Mr. Johnson, you've had a rough four days, but I think the worst is behind you."

"Four days?" I said. " I thought I just had a nightmare."

The doctor was grim now. "You had a nightmare alright, from what we could tell," he said. "What's with the key you wanted from your wallet?" he asked. "We finally found it, and you clutched it in your hand."

I answered him, "Doctor, that's the only thing from my former life that I have."

Dr. Williams said, "I'm so glad to see the progress today. I'll order a soft diet for you tonight," he went on. "I imagine Dr. Sherman will see you tomorrow."

I liked Dr. Sherman at once. She was tall with soft gray hair.

"I've been here twenty-seven years," she told me. "I think you'll like the staff. We have around five or six patients at a time." She told me the routine. "Day after tomorrow you'll leave this room and be in more of a group setting. We'll start with you meeting the others, then you'll join our group sessions, where you'll make real progress."

CHAPTER FOURTEEN

The new quarters were nice, kinda like a camp. My bed was better. I had a nice shower, and good pj's and sandals.

First thing, I did was get a long, hot shower. Dr. Sherman told me to be in the community room at two o'clock.

I was apparently the last one to get there. Three men and one young woman were sitting in a circle with Dr. Sherman. She said, "Come in, Bob, we use first names here." She introduced them, "Theresa, Ray, Alan and Clyde." They looked so young and somewhat defeated.

Dr. Sherman asked me to tell any of my story I would like to. "Well," I said, "to make a long story short, I had some kind of accident, and I have amnesia."

I heard a couple of gasps and some feet shuffling around. I went on, "I don't remember who I am or where I'm from. I was found on the river bank in pretty bad shape."

I glanced at each of them. They were staring at me in amazement. "I've tried everything I know to find my identity." I sighed, looking at the floor.

"I got a prescription of opiates for my headaches, started abusing them, drinking and smoking weed." I looked up at Dr. Sherman. "Then I really got with the wrong person, smoked something … I don't know what, and here I am."

No one spoke. Finally Dr. Sherman went on with the meeting, talking with everyone. A chaplain came in and read Bible verses and prayed.

Why did I know every verse? It was all so familiar.

The community room had some games and a TV. The men asked me to join them in a game of poker, but Dr. Sherman said I would be seeing Dr. Williams in my room shortly.

Teresa turned on the TV and curled her bony legs under her.

It wasn't Dr. Williams, but a nurse who came in, carrying a syringe. "Here's your life-saver injection. You'll only have this one. Roll over Mr. Johnson."

I didn't react when I heard it this time. "Oh, yes," she added. "Your parents were here to see you. I explained you can't have guests until the end of your program."

I had been thinking of Leonard and Grace for two days, dreading what to say to them. I would just move out.

The days became routine – the group therapy, the chaplain, good food we didn't have to eat in bed. Clyde was discharged and two women were admitted. I was seeing what a roller-coaster it really was. We saw movies and answered questions, slowly working through our problems, promising ourselves, "Never again."

At the end of my third week, the sheriff was allowed to see me. "Boy," he grinned and shook my hand. "You look like a different feller. How much weight have you gained?"

"I'm proud to say six pounds as of this morning," I answered. We eat like pigs around here."

"Well," he looked serious now, "Dr. Sherman tells me you're doing well, but she wants you to see her weekly for two or three months after you're discharged." He went on, "and Gus is anxious to get you back."

I have not felt so light and happy since … well, I can't remember, I thought to myself.

CHAPTER FIFTEEN

I was discharged right on time and set up ten appointments with Dr. Sherman. I went back to work and got right into the swing of things.

The guys were so glad to see me, telling me how great I looked. I explained I couldn't go to C.J.'s for a while. I left the impression it was just a matter of time. But I knew it would be *'Never Again.'*

I asked Leonard and Grace "Please give me a little time, then I'll tell the whole story."

They both hugged me and pretended nothing ever happened.

I joined the gym and worked out most afternoons. I loved the feeling of getting stronger. I did more than my quota at work. I kept every appointment with Dr. Sherman. She was the greatest.

She convinced me, "You may never regain your total memory, Bob." She was speaking softly in her darkened room. "I do, however, believe your dreams are connected to your past life."

"Believe me, Bob, you can make a new life. You are making a wonderful start."

I knew it was true, and all up to me.

At my last appointment, I brought her flowers, hugged her and cried a little.

She did too.

CHAPTER SIXTEEN

I marked off my calendar each day. It seems nobody is looking for me. I had "the dream" often. Leonard and Grace turned eighty.

I dated a couple of women from work. One especially attracted me. She had dark hair and eyes. She lied to me about being unmarried. Her husband returned from California and she had to confess.

Leonard wasn't able to care for the stock any longer. After much discussion and a few tears, Nanny was sold to the 4-H leader for breeding. A neighbor took the chickens and 'Ol Jack went to live at a petting zoo where he gets lots of love.

Leonard and Grace spent most of their time in their chairs with the TV blaring. I helped as much as I could, bringing take-out food or sometimes making chili. *Where did I learn to make chili?* I wondered.

I was still having the same dream.

Would I ever know who I am? Apparently no one missed or wanted me.

Leonard and Grace made a new will. They left everything … It wasn't much … to Hope, Robert's daughter. She was grown up now.

Leonard called Nicole, his ex-daughter-in-law and asked her, "Please Nicole, bring Roberta Hope to see us."

Nicole did come the next Sunday. Hope was shy, she barely remembered her grandparents. The visit was short, Leonard gave Hope a copy of the will. She barely hugged them goodbye. It was the last time they would ever see her.

Leonard had a stroke ten days later and only lived a few days. His funeral service was at the community church. It was packed with friends and neighbors. Everyone loved Leonard. I helped Grace up to the coffin. She looked at him as though she had no idea who he was. It broke my heart.

Three weeks later, Nicole and Hope had found a nursing home for Grace and had a For Sale sign in front of the house.

I packed my things, and took the hand-made quilt from my bed. I knew Grace would want me to have it. I loaded the TV and microwave in the back seat and roped the Yamaha in the back. On my way out, I picked up the old guitar and put it in the truck. Before I drove to Careyville, I made a last trip to visit the only Dad I could ever remember. I talked to him for a long time about all the great times we had together, and cried my eyes out.

The nursing home was on my way. I wanted to hug Grace and tell her how much I loved her. The hazel eyes lit up when she saw me. "Robert, did you stay for practice?"

I knew right away. I went along with her, hugged and kissed her.

I didn't look back.

CHAPTER SEVENTEEN

Bob Johnson was alone in the world.

I found a pretty nice studio apartment in Careyville. My friends at work thought it would be fun to have a house-warming party. They filled my little apartment, drinking beer and eating pizza. They actually brought me about everything I needed.

I had "the dream" again.

I grew a beard and let my hair grow long. I got acquainted with a waitress at Annie's Cafe named Rachel. She was nice enough looking with dirty blond hair, pale blue eyes and almost as tall as me.

We went to the movies, or maybe watched a movie at my place, just casual things. Sometimes she would spend the night.

Rachel had been married twice and neither of us wanted anything serious.

I had been promoted to inspector.

Gus Wicke retired, and a transfer manager from another factory in a town called Cloverdale, somewhere in the middle of the state, took over. I didn't get along with him right from the start, so when I was offered a position in Cloverdale, I jumped at it. I said so long to my friends, kissed Rachel goodbye and good luck.

I packed my few belongings and hit the road. Bob Johnson is starting a new chapter. Bob had good traveling the first day. He had a light feeling, *I'll make a new life for myself,* he thought, *might even get married.* He chuckled to himself. He slept soundly that night, but wasn't up to eating breakfast for some reason. *That's not like me,* he thought.

He took a cup of coffee and set out. *I'll get there by dark,* he said to himself. Bob turned on the radio and concentrated on the traffic.

He had a slight ache in his belly. "Guess I should eat something," he mumbled. He reached into the console and dug out an old pack of cheese crackers, opened a bottle of water and washed them down.

Bob drove on for a few hours. He didn't want any lunch, the pain was a little worse. It was almost dark when Bob saw the Cloverdale City Limits sign.

He stopped at the first hotel. Bob sat in a tub of hot water for a long time, trying to ease that nagging pain. He didn't sleep, just doubled up in the fetal position and moaned a little. *I may have to get something done about this,* he thought.

Bob put on the same clothes he left Careyville in, not bothering to put his shirt-tail in. *It hurts to walk now,* he thought. Bob made it to the lobby, picked up the daily paper and went back to his room. "I'll see what's happening in Cloverdale," he said aloud. It was the last thought Bob Johnson ever had.

The front page was a story about the Cloverdale Middle School girls winning the championship soccer match with a huge picture of the coach and her team in color. The headline read, "Faye Hollister, coach of Cloverdale Middle School girls soccer team, takes her team to the state finals, and wins."

He felt the room swimming around him and fainted dead away. When he came to, the pain was bad in his right side and he felt feverish.

"I know who I am," he said to the empty room. "I'm Zach Hollister and this is my wife!" He felt like vomiting and tried, but didn't. "She's still Faye Hollister. I know where I live – the house in my dreams." He took the key from his wallet and kissed it. "My house key. I wonder if she still lives there?"

In spite of the pain, he made it to his truck. Everything was familiar. It was as though he was in a clear bubble, looking at everything new. It was the same streets, though not quite the same.

When he turned onto Windmill Lane, his heart was pounding and his head was hot. The house looked the same, the crepe myrtle the same, the river the same.

I wonder if anyone lives here? he thought.

It was dark and quiet. He put the key in the lock, turned it and walked into the living room, trying not to collapse. He stood for several seconds, his eyes adjusting to the dark.

He could see her now, in the dining room. "My Faye, my wife," he whispered.

He started to speak to her when suddenly she was screaming, throwing hot coffee on him. He teetered toward her, trying to speak. He felt her hand, the room spinning around him. He went down hard.

CHAPTER EIGHTEEN

The EMT's ran into the house with medical bags and a gurney. Faye related what had happened as they got busy, taking vitals and starting an IV. As the medic pulled up the man's shirt sleeve to start the IV, she saw it … a butterfly tattoo on his arm.

It was a good thing Faye had sat down. "That's Zach!" she screamed, "That's my husband!"

The men looked at her as though she were hysterical. He'd been missing for over two years.

"Okay, lady," the medic said. "This man is critically ill. We've got to get him to the hospital, stat." In no time, the sirens were screaming down the street. Faye couldn't move. Her head was swimming. She put her head on the cool table and stayed there for several minutes.

How's this happening? she thought. *Where has Zach been? Why does he look like that? Has he been in jail?* She regained enough sense to call Cindy. "Cindy, are you free to drive me somewhere? Something has happened, I'll tell you on the way."

Cindy said, "Mother has Easton today. I'll be right there."

In halting terms, Faye tried to fill Cindy in on the weird happenings of the morning. Cindy was speechless too. She reached for Faye's hand, "All our prayers have been answered."

Faye ran into the ER like a wild person. "Where's the man the ambulance just brought in?" she shouted at the woman behind the desk.

"Are you a relative?" the woman calmly asked.

"I'm his wife." Faye was on the verge of hysteria.

Cindy caught up with Faye and put her arm around her. "He's down this hall in room four; only one person allowed," the woman said.

Cindy headed Faye down the hall and said, "I'll be waiting right out here, Honey."

"Oh, my word, Cindy," Faye cried out, "Call Zach's mom and dad, and Phil. Then maybe – just call Phil and he can break the news in person."

A doctor was coming out of room four. "Doctor, I'm that mans' wife. How is he?"

"Oh, Mrs. Johnson, he's gone to surgery." He looked at her shocked face.

"Doctor, I mean the man the ambulance brought from Windmill Lane." Faye said, totally confused now.

"Yes, he has a ruptured appendix. Excuse me, I'm needed in OR," the doctor was practically running.

Faye went back to Cindy and told her what was going on. "The doctor called me Mrs. Johnson."

Cindy said, "Let's ask the desk nurse about his name."

"Yes," the nurse answered, "Bob Johnson, from Careyville." Here, I made a copy of his I.D."

Faye studied the copy for several seconds, "It's Zach. It's Zach, the way he looked the last time I saw him."

Her voice was only a whisper. She was about to collapse when Cindy put a chair under her. "You'll get to the bottom of it later. Right now, we'll pray for good news."

"Where is the OR?" Cindy asked the nurse. The nurse directed them to the elevator. They stopped at the nurse's station and were directed to the waiting room.

"Someone will talk to you soon, Mrs. Johnson."

Cindy called her mother about Easton. Her mother had to leave soon. Cindy told Faye, "I have to leave soon, do I need to get you anything?"

Faye asked for a bottle of water. As Cindy handed it to her, Faye said, "Oh, Angel is locked in the bedroom, Cindy."

"Don't worry, Honey, I'm on my way."

As Cindy got on the elevator, Zach's folks were getting off, their faces white, totally in shock, running down the hall. They saw Faye, slumped back in a chair. Everyone was talking at once. Faye told them everything so far. They all cried, rejoiced and prayed.

It was over two hours before the doctor came into the waiting room and asked for the Johnson family. Faye answered, "Yes, I'm his wife."

"Your husband is in I.C.U, Mrs. Johnson. He's in critical condition. Apparently, his appendix has been ruptured for a while."

"Will he be OK?" Faye interrupted.

"Time will tell. I can give you more after twenty-four hours."

"When can we see him?" Zach's dad asked.

"Talk to the desk nurse. She'll tell you the restrictions." And he was gone.

They all sat quiet, still numb with disbelief. Finally, Phil went to talk to the nurse. He came back and said, "One person can go in every four hours, but no one for a while." Phil said, "Does anyone want coffee? Here's a coffee maker for us."

"I'll make it," Sarah stood up. "We could all use a cup."

Hours went by before a nurse stepped in and said, "Someone can see Mr. Johnson now. Don't try to talk to him and don't stay more than five minutes." Faye entered the I.C.U. room. Zach was hooked to beeping machines, his face white on the pillows, still asleep.

She just stood there, shaking and trying to see Zach through the beard. *Yes,* she said to herself, *That's definitely my Zach. But where has he been? What has he been through? Who has he been with? And why is he using the name "Bob Johnson"?*

The family took turns seeing Zach. Friends heard the news and brought snacks and prayed with the family.

Zach began to rouse a little on the second day. The doctor told the family, "It looks as though he'll make a full recovery with time and T.L.C." Faye assured him she would see to that. On the third afternoon, Zach was moved to his own room.

It was wonderful. He could talk some now, but the family didn't press him for answers. There would be time for that later. They kissed him, welcomed him "home" told him, "We'll celebrate later," and everyone left except Faye.

She took Zach's hand and said quietly, "I'll be back soon, Darling."

Phil drove Faye home and assured her he would take care of Angel.

She packed a few things, showered, got into some comfortable clothes, grabbed a pillow and blanket and went back to the hospital in about an hour.

Zach was asleep and didn't respond to her. Faye settled down in the reclining chair and turned on the TV with the volume very low. She fell right to sleep, awakened only when the nurses came in every few hours for blood or to change Zach's IV.

The next morning Zach got soft food for breakfast. Faye raised his head a little and fed him, neither of them making conversation.

That afternoon, Faye was sitting quietly when she heard Zach move around. "Hawkeye," he said weakly.

Faye jumped up, "What do you need, darling?"

"I would like a bath, and a shave."

Faye called the nurse's station and soon an orderly was there to clean Zach up. While the bath was going on, Faye went to the cafeteria for some food. She watched the other people who, like her, looked tired and anxious. *What will happen to us now?* she wondered. *How could it ever be the same?*

When she returned to Zach's room and walked in, he was sitting up in bed, grinning at her. "What do you think, now, Hawkeye? Do you know me now?"

Faye couldn't help herself, she cried, and had to sit down. "Zach, you hardly look a day older."

That evening, several people dropped by, only staying a minute or two.

Zach's dad said, "Son, you're a sensation. The TV station wants to interview someone."

A shocked look came on Zach's face. "I have to talk to Faye first," he said.

The next day after the morning routine of meds and tests, Zach asked Faye if she was ready to hear his story.

"I think so," she whispered and pulled a chair up to the bed and took his hand. It took all day between interruptions. Faye didn't ask any questions, just let Zach take his time. It was the most remarkable and also unbelievable story anyone ever could hear. He didn't leave anything out, his memory was clear. He was exhausted.

Faye thanked him for answering the questions she had wondered for years. She kissed his forehead, "I'm going home. I guess Angel thinks I've died. Tomorrow, I'll tell you about my two years."

That night she couldn't sleep. Thinking about Zach with other women made her heart ache. *But I have to be realistic,* she thought. *He didn't even know he had a wife; he didn't even know who he really was.* But it still hurt.

The next day she did tell Zach everything, beginning with the search of the river.

"Where's my truck and boat?" he interrupted.

"Your truck is in the garage, and your boat was never found," Faye said, seeing the disappointment on his face.

"I got my teachers certificate, and I coach girls soccer. It's kept me busy."

"No boyfriends?" Zach asked without looking at her.

"Oh, I went to a couple of 'single-mingles' but I couldn't get interested."

Zach looked at her with those big green eyes and just said, "Good."

Phil called about then and told Faye, "There's someone here from an Atlanta newspaper asking questions about my missing brother. What do you want me to tell him?"

"Just tell him what little you know," Faye answered.

"It's in the local paper too, talk of the town," Phil replied. "He's a celebrity."

Zach was discharged the next day. Drew helped get him in the house and to the couch.

"Boy, this smells like home." Zach was looking around. Nothing much had changed except the blinds on the big windows. Faye made up the bed in the guest room.

When she came through carrying some of Zach's old clothes, he couldn't believe it. "You mean you kept my clothes all these years?" he asked.

"Oh, I thought of donating them plenty of times, but something wouldn't let me. Sometimes, I would hold one of your shirts and dance with it."

He had a lump in his throat. *What she must have gone through. Somehow, I'll make it up to her,* he promised himself.

Faye took good care of him and could see him getting stronger. Angel smelled him for two days before she would allow him to touch her. Now she's right at his feet.

Zach and Faye gave an interview to the TV station, then a national network called. They would pay for pictures and the story. Zach said no, not right now, maybe later.

He grew stronger and was doing things around the house. He bought a battery for his pick up and drove to the dealership alone. It was old-boys day, all the crew asking questions at once. He decided to surprise Faye and stopped at the barber shop for a haircut.

The evenings were cool now. Faye had the fireplace on and was picking out a movie when he came home. She squealed with delight when she saw him and without thinking, threw her arms around him.

"Now it's really you," she screamed. She backed away, feeling kinda foolish. They had awkwardly avoided touching one another.

"I ordered a pizza" she said. "I had a long day at the school. Thought we might watch a movie."

"Sounds good to me," Zach said.

While Faye paid the delivery man, Zach was going through the movies. He started one and sat down with a slice of pizza. "I got us a good one, Hawkeye, since it's almost Halloween, it's one called *Ghost*. Faye felt weak all of a sudden, but didn't say anything. They ate in silence, as the movie went on. Once Zach said quietly, "This isn't a scary movie."

Toward the end of the movie, Zach heard Faye sniffling and glanced over at her. She had tears running down her cheeks. Instinctively, he reached over, turned her face to him, took his knuckle and wiped the tears. Suddenly he was running his fingers through her silky black hair, then he was gently touching her ear, then her neck.

Faye moved against him, a shiver going over her, she lifted her face to him. He kissed her long and deep. Faye took his hands and lead him to their bed.

The next morning, they were still in each other's arms, neither wanting to move. This could be one of the happiest days ever for Zach and Faye.

But two things would change all that.

After breakfast, Faye received a call from the insurance agent who had settled the claim on Zach's policy last May.

"Mrs. Hollister, I understand your husband has returned, is that correct?" he said firmly.

"Uh, yes he has," Faye mumbled, thoughts going through her head in a jumble.

The agent said, "Mrs. Hollister, under the circumstances, the underwriter expects a refund of the hundred thousand dollars within ten business days."

Faye was practically speechless. "Uh, of course, I'll be in touch later."

She and Zach sat at the table taking it in.

"Do you have that much?" Zach asked.

"Lord, no," Faye looked at him. "Do you have any money?"

"A coupla hundred," he looked almost ashamed.

She said. "Soon you can go back to work and we'll be okay."

But the mail delivery brought more news, not good. Zach's hospital bills were beginning to come in. Within four days, there were over two hundred thousand dollars in bills. They thought about selling the trucks, a second mortgage, or asking family for help.

Zach said, "I know Mom and Dad don't have it, and I wouldn't ask them anyway."

Zach went back to work. *I'll make payments on the hospital bills until it's all paid,* he thought. *After all, they saved my life.*

But fate had something else in store for them. The following week, one afternoon late, two strangers rang the doorbell. Zach and Faye were barely home from work.

"I'll get it." Zach opened the door.

One of the men, tall and thin, spoke, "I'm Glen Walden and this is Kenneth White. Are you Zach Hollister?" he asked in a New York accent.

"Yes. I am Zach. What can I do for you?" Zach immediately thought of the hundred thousand dollars when he saw a briefcase.

"We're from Bendle Productions," Mr. Walden answered. "We'd like to talk with you and your wife about buying the rights to your unbelievable story."

For a minute, Zach couldn't speak.

Faye came up beside him. "Ask them in, Zach," she said.

Zach and Faye were completely dumbfounded when they heard the proposal. It would care for them for life.

Mr. Walden and Mr. White wanted to hear some of the story. Faye made coffee, and three hours later the papers were signed. They would be paid within three days. Next year, their story would be a made for TV movie.

Zach and Faye didn't sleep that night. They called Zach's family and Cindy and Drew. Soon the house was full with laughter and disbelief. And, "You're millionaires!" from everyone.

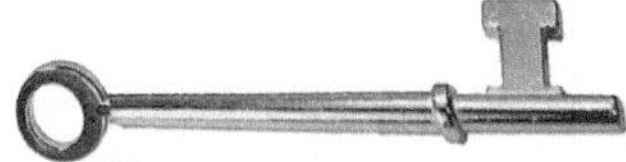

FINAL

Zach squeezed Faye's hand and looked in her eyes, "What are you thinking?" he asked. They were buckled in their seats, the plane taxiing down the runway.

"How would you like to have a baby?" she whispered.

"It's a good thing we're having this honeymoon in Hawaii now," he grinned, and kissed her long and deep.

ABOUT THE AUTHOR

C. J. Johns lives in Georgetown, Tennessee, with her golden retriever, Angel. *She says, "Key to the Dream* got into my head like an old song and would not leave. I hope you enjoy reading this as much as I enjoyed writing it."

Johns grew up and married in West Texas. After her husband died young, she moved her family back to her native Tennessee. For the next fifty-five years, she owned and successfully operated five businesses in Bradley County, Tennessee. She is a descendant of "Devil Anse Hatfield" of the "Hatfield and McCoy" feud.

Myriad Pro and Ironwood on 50# S Archival Crème White
Type and design by Karen Paul Stone